then there was NIV

where fairy tales end and reality begins

Printed in the United States of America.

ISBN: 978-1-59571-421-3
LIBRARY OF CONGRESS NUMBER: 2009931563

Designed and published by

Word Association Publishers
205 Fifth Avenue
Tarentum, Pennsylvania 15084

www.wordassociation.com
1 800 827 7903

then there was NIV

where fairy tales end and reality begins

Janice Blair

THIS BOOK IS DEDICATED TO THE LORD, WHO HAS GIVEN ME MORE THAN I HAVE EVER HOPED OR DREAMED.

And a special thanks for all your love and support always to Jan, Jessica, & Jean.

And to my twin, Joyce.

PRELUDE

What happens when an overbearing boss,

Ted Strain, challenges Daisy with a short deadline for a story?

Enjoy the adventure as Daisy's life unfolds after the

unexpected happens, when the fairy tale ends and reality

begins. Be assured, in the midst of all of our planning

—life happens.

Table of Contents

Chapter One

THE FALL

FOUR-YEAR-OLD BRADEN, excited to visit his daddy at work, scurried about the reception area of the fifteenth floor of the Benson Building. In the deep pocket of his slicker was hidden a yellow number-two pencil he had taken from his Grandmother's open bible. During her early morning devotion, she had fallen asleep in her recliner. Braden had stood on his tippy toes to kiss her goodbye and this is when he had snatched the forbidden sharp object from the book on her lap. Now he hummed and smiled as he thought about his mother's promise to take him and his baby sister to the downtown library. Tucked under his arm, he carried his favorite picture book about an owl named Spotty.

While his mother held his two-year-old sister and conversed with Bekki the receptionist, a woman in a tailored suit barged up to the desk interrupting their conversation. Braden could tell this displeased his mother.

He listened as the receptionist said to the impatient woman, "Just a moment and I will page Mr. Strain for you, please."

Braden noticed that the woman didn't acknowledge his mother. She turned in his direction, placed her hands on her hips, and began to tap her high-heeled shoe. He smiled and asked her, "Wanna look at my picture book?"

Without responding, Bekki gave Braden a disdainful look. A buzzer on the desk sounded and she said, "Mr. Strain is ready to see you now."

The woman nodded and said, "Thank you," as she proceeded into the inner office corridor with her navy blue heels clicking the hard-surfaced floor.

"Well," said Braden's mother, "some people are so rude and are in such a hurry these days. She acted as though we were invisible." Braden smiled up at her as she tousled his full head of hair.

He continued to explore the foyer as Bekki paged his daddy's office.

After the short visit as the three waited for the elevator, his mother ran into an old friend. She became engrossed in conversation and Braden stole away as a person exited the fifteenth floor stairwell. His mother saw him out of the corner of her eye and went to retrieve him from the stairwell. By the time she reached him, he had hopped down the first flight of stairs.

"Braden, you come up here this instant. Young man, you know you are not allowed to leave my side when we are in this building."

"Okay Mommy," Braden called as he hopped up the flight

of stairs. His mother held onto his sister, opened the heavy door, and waited as Braden made it to the top step. They didn't see or hear the yellow number-two pencil fall from his slicker pocket and roll down onto the cement steps.

Ted Strain greeted Daisy and jumped right into the meeting's topic. "Ms. Zookes, you have had six weeks to work on this adventure story and you show up at my office empty handed. With only six more weeks remaining to deliver the adventure story manuscript, I do hope you have a plan of action? If you drop the ball on this assignment your employment with this company could come into question."

Daisy squirmed inwardly but maintained a calm outer appearance. She knew a sign of weakness would only fuel Ted's ego. Since he used her proper name instead of calling her Daisy, she recognized his tactics to show his displeasure and authority. He had a supercharged ego since his promotion to Editor-in-Chief of the Hannah and Rhutkers JC Publishing Company.

Daisy scanned the peculiar artifacts atop his large glass top, mahogany desk and fibbed, "Don't worry Ted, I mean Mr. Strain, I do have a few ideas and some notes put together on my computer for the story." She hadn't even begun to work on the story and she disliked being berated by him.

She began to ponder while he ranted on. Had it been six weeks since Strain had first approached her about doing an adventure story? She remembered briefing him earlier about the difficulties she faced with this project. Her forte consisted of stories about real people and real places, not made up adventure flicks to entertain adolescent readers. Strain seemed oblivious to this fact. He had quizzed her about how hard could it be to put together an adventure story for an adolescent publication series? Meanwhile, his attitude did nothing to enlighten her.

Strain interrupted her thoughts, "Are you listening to me, Daisy?"

"Umm…yes. Sorry, I had been thinking of more story lines and ideas to add as you were speaking. This story has been fun to develop."

"Good, then e-mail me your story outline on Friday. Oh, and here are some action books I read as a youngster. Perhaps they can be of some help." Ted handed her three hardcover volumes of books with worn covers and yellowing pages. Scanning the title pages, she could see they were a young person's reading material.

As she exited his office, she reassured Strain the adventure story would be completed on the agreed-upon deadline.

Daisy grimaced as she walked down the hall, glad to have this difficult meeting with Ted over. His early morning e-mail had set the tone for the meeting. She knew it had been foolish to believe this project would have fallen by the wayside. Stupefied, she wished she had prepared some notes in advance. Daisy berated herself thinking, "Telling one fib after another gave the appearance of being disorganized. I must have looked scattered and unprofessional to Ted. As she passed Bekki in the reception area, she thought, "Plus, running into the mother with her two children at the receptionist's desk infuriated me. I can't understand how some women with so much free time would simply want to visit their husbands at work. Don't they have something better to do?"

Seeing all three elevators engaged, Daisy decided to take the stairs to her eleventh- floor cubicle. She entered the stairwell and hurried down the flight of steps when the unthinkable happened. Braden's yellow number-two pencil lay parallel on the fourth cement step. Carrying the books and lost in thought, she noticed it, too late. Her navy blue, high-heeled foot came down on the pencil, causing her to slip sideways. Slamming her head on the metal strip of the concrete step, her body continued to lunge forward.

Since most people used the elevator, no one heard the sound of fright escaping from her throat right before she hit her head on the metal edge of the step. This initial hit rendered her unconscious, and then she resembled a rag doll being tossed down the steps.

About twenty minutes later an associate named Tom Nimbleton entered the Benson Building stairwell. Returning to his fifteenth floor office, he had bought a cup of coffee from the Filter n' Cup coffee shop. Tom used the stairs instead of the elevator as he strove to keep his weight and physique in impeccable shape. He took great pride in this daily routine of conquering the fifteen flights of stairs. Whistling a radio tune he had heard during his morning commute, he took the steps two at a time. On his way up the stairwell, he remembered a memo he had to retrieve from Ted Strain's secretary. With the memo on his mind he continued his stair climbing ritual.

He came upon Daisy's limp, motionless body sprawled on the cold, concrete mid-landing of the fourteenth floor. Tom analyzed how she must have fallen and had come to rest on this mid-landing section. Apprehensively, Tom observed Daisy's unconscious, injured body in the stillness of the stairwell. He viewed a gaping, bloody wound on the front of her forehead, blood staining her torn navy blue, tailored jacket and her white blouse. One of her high-heeled shoes lay angled on its side in the corner of the landing and the books she had carried were strewn about. Tom knew by the pale pallor of Daisy's skin tone and her shallow, inconsistent breathing that her injuries were grave. He dared not move her. Placing his coffee cup on the concrete floor, he knelt to feel for a pulse while speaking her name.

He recognized Daisy and also knew her good friend Darla from the Michelangelo's Ice Cream Parlor where he took his wife for a treat on a date.

Feeling a weak pulse and without a response to her name, he retreated a few steps to the twelfth floor.

"Call 911," Tom told a woman seated at the first cubicle, "a female employee has hurt herself. She's bleeding and unconscious on the fourteen floor landing of the stairwell." Tom then commandeered a man seated in the next cubicle to assist him. Hearing the urgency in Tom's voice and seeing the determination in his eyes, they both did as he instructed.

Chapter Two:

MIRROR LAKE

Lying on her back, Daisy opened her eyes and looked at the bluest sky she had ever seen. Startled, she sat up. Lush, green grass bordered a large, tranquil lake. She noted the temperature seemed right for walking or for lazing about in a hammock with a good book. She scanned the countryside, wondering how she had come to be lying here. It appeared to be a peaceful place as she breathed in the fresh invigorating air. Taking another deep breath, she found it even more refreshing to her now awakened senses. The air she breathed in pacified her mounting anxiety. Still perplexed, she thought it out of the ordinary to have been sleeping, because she preferred not to take naps during the middle of the day.

"That's strange," she said out loud, as she wondered what had become of her navy blue suit. She remembered putting it on for work that morning. Now she wore her white chiffon blouse and tan khaki pants, accompanied by her comfortable penny loafers.

Massaging her temples, her head ached as she wondered

again how she came to be here. Beginning to feel anxious, she calmed her nerves with reassuring words and focusing on the task at hand. She assessed no imminent danger or hostile environment within her surroundings. It looked as if she were on a holiday. She chided herself with the fact that she should be at work developing the adventure story for her boss Ted Strain.

She laughed as she considered Ted's mover and shaker image. He had the very qualities she desired in a male companion, but the thought of dating someone as demanding and roguish as him made her stomach turn. He had been her boss as the Editor-in-Chief of the Hannah and Rhutkers JC Publishing Company since she started working during her junior year of college at the Indianapolis Writers Institute. His brownish, maroon suits accompanied by starched white shirts and no-nonsense ties added to his overbearing stature. She pictured his thick dark wavy hair graying at the temples, along with his bushy eyebrows that remained bent in towards his nose, all of which made him look as though he were brooding about something. Daisy and her co-worker friend, Darla Mae Firkens, called him Mr. Pain whenever they referred to him in private conversation.

Her mind pictured Darla working at her cubicle while taking another look at the tranquil lake. Darla's cubicle was adjacent to hers on the eleventh floor, while Strain's mega office stood on the fifteenth floor where he directed his often ridiculous, overbearing demands.

Needless to say, Daisy took a serious approach to work; when a report or story deadline was due, she could be counted on. She considered loafing about the countryside, dressed in casual clothing as a sign of slothfulness. Her normal business attire consisted of expensive suits, accessorized with matching shoes, purses, and jewelry. One thing could be said of Ms. Delores Anne Zookes, alias Daisy: fashion and style were a top priority. Her professional attire worked well for the prestige needed in her journalistic career. The female office circle envied her sense of style and fashion.

A memory flashed through her mind. Daisy remembered spilling water onto her expensive navy blue suit and tailored white blouse. She had just left Strain's office after a heated discussion. She had been reassuring him she would have the adventure story completed by the twelve-week deadline.

Strain had made a contract with publicist Gloria Davenport of the "Adolescents-do-Read" Organization to provide an adventure story for her magazine publication. This deal came about at an afternoon luncheon honoring Daisy and a group of co-workers for their outstanding literary and journalistic accomplishments. At the luncheon, Strain had personally toasted Daisy for the numerous articles she supplied for his various contacts in the publishing world.

Davenport had approached Strain during the luncheon asking if one of his prize writers could provide her firm with an adolescent adventure story. Strain boasted and assured

Davenport that his writers were more than capable of providing such a story.

Today at the meeting, Strain had been berating Daisy on her slow progress in developing a story. Six weeks had already passed since he volunteered her for the project. Daisy thought this venture with Davenport would fizzle out, as several other deals had done in the past. Strain kept many projects and opportunities in the fire. He made it a common practice of committing his staff to excessive writing jobs, only to have many of the deals fizzle out way before the deadlines. Shocked and tongue-tied, Daisy realized this was not to be the case concerning this story. Strain expected her to deliver an adolescent adventure story within the six remaining weeks.

In further retrospection, Daisy knew it was Tuesday morning and that she had stopped by the water cooler outside his office door to douse her parched throat and to clear her mind. She had fumbled with the cheap and flimsy cups supplied by the Rollin's Water Company, thus wetting her suit. She smirked as a thought went through her mind comparing the cups to the cheap and flimsy behavior Strain often resorted to at outside office functions. Daisy remembered wracking her brain for a creative idea for the adventure story as she tossed the empty cup into the trash receptacle and proceeded to the elevators. After that, her mind drew a blank and she couldn't remember anything further from this point on. Now, she found herself lounging next to a lake dressed in casual clothes.

Alone and without her purse, Daisy became more dismayed and frightened. She carried her cell phone, car keys, and credit cards in her purse. Without these essential lifelines came a feeling of inadequacy and vulnerability. Once more she had to calm herself and try not to succumb to a mounting fear of the unknown. In the stillness of the moment, she scanned the vicinity hoping to see a car, some people, birds, anything. The quiet disturbed her. Gazing off in the distance she saw only the rolling hills of green grass, the blue skies, a few far away mountains, and the still, tranquil lake. Absent were billboards, signs, trees, people, and animals. She saw only the surreal lake.

Daisy ambled over to the lake and stared at her reflection in the clear, untouched water. She took comfort seeing at least her appearance remained intact. As she studied her reflection, her simple studded earrings glistened and she noted the lightweight gold chain about her neck.

Her good friend Paul Thornchen had given her the gold chain. Paul held to high morals and made it a practice of going to church every Sunday. His genteel, soft demeanor set him apart from most men she dated. Sometimes he took her out to dinner and a movie, which she did enjoy. But still, she thought Paul lived in the slow lane, while she gravitated towards people who were the fast movers and shakers—dominant individuals who desired to run things and who wanted to earn lots of money. Paul seemed content with what he had. She had little interest in that type of lethargic mentality. However, Paul's handsome face and good physique caused most women to look twice and smile at him when they were out on a date. Daisy thought warm thoughts of him as she fondled the delicate gold chain around her neck.

Studying the calm, mesmerizing water, she hesitated to touch it. But when she did, the ripples spread out as a melody of a tuned flute. On instinct, she smelled the water, checking to see if it might be foul or polluted. Drawn to the water, she had an urge to drink and taste this pure, clean water. Perhaps it seemed silly, but she drank at least four large double handfuls of water. Then she reclined and took another deep breath. She gazed to the right and spied a large sign indicating "Mirror Lake."

Why hadn't she noticed the large, white sign with its dark green letters outlined in gold before? The sign stood about fifty yards away and seemed to have appeared out of nowhere. Baffled, Daisy rinsed her face hoping the cool water would help to ease her mind and clear her senses. Unable to recollect a place called Mirror Lake, she read the sign again.

Nearby, a school of fish swam by the lake's edge. The fish were multicolored with all the colors of the rainbow tattooed within their scales. She watched as they played and swam together, unafraid of her nearness. Watching them brought a deeper sense of curiosity about this place and how she had come to be here. In spite of her uncertainty, a peace and calmness started to engulf her.

After splashing more water onto her face, Daisy turned and walked away from Mirror Lake. She reasoned that if she stayed put, the possibility existed that nothing would happen. She wanted to get back to her work, to her apartment, and to her life. Having geared her life to living in the fast lane, she'd go crazy remaining in this slow paced scenario. Determined to find out her whereabouts, she began to explore the area.

Chapter Three:

BIG BOB

Station Nineteen of the Monroe County Fire and Rescue Unit responded to the dispatcher's 911 call. The call relayed to the team that a woman had been found unconscious and bleeding with apparent blunt trauma to the head in a stairwell at the downtown Indianapolis Benson Building. The paramedic team sprang into action driving their emergency transports to the scene of the accident. The Benson Building stood in the heart of downtown Indianapolis on Peridion Street close to the Circle City War Monument. The heavy traffic around the city's circle made it difficult to maneuver the larger medical transport vehicles. Due to frequent occurrences, most of the sidewalk pedestrians showed little if any interest at the sight of the emergency vehicles.

Big Bob Carnicom, the head paramedic, disembarked from the light green Freightliner Medic Master vehicle and gazed up at the towering Benson Building. Designed with a romantic exterior, this impressive granite building stood eighteen stories high with massive pillars accentuating the top three stories. The paramedic team entered the building, following a doorman who awaited their arrival. They used the elevators to reach the twelfth floor and then entered the stairwell for the remaining few steps. Big Bob sensed an air of urgency among the maze of cubicles across from the east stairwell. The Hannah and Rhutkers JC Publishing Company employees became alive with curiosity as the emergency vehicles and crew arrived and entered the building. The paramedic team had a job to do, and they did not waste time for idle chats or nosy inquisitors. In their line of work, every second counted.

Upon entering the stairwell, Big Bob questioned Tom Nimbleton, who had remained by Daisy's side. As the paramedics assessed Daisy's condition, they took the necessary precaution of placing a neck brace to stabilize her, thus preventing further spinal or neck injuries. With care, they straightened her bent legs and twisted arms while checking for contusions and broken bones. Tom had placed a blanket over Daisy to keep her warm because she had displayed signs of shock.

Daisy had sustained injuries in her fall needing treatment by a skilled physician as soon as possible or she might not regain consciousness. Big Bob had made this immediate observation of her condition. A non-frivolous man who had been a paramedic for over 26 years, his crew took all instructions from him and relied heavily on his observations. He had a keen sense for imminent medical treatment. He had an office filled with plaques, awards, and gifts testifying to his capabilities. These were a meager tribute to the lives he had helped save. Today, Delores Anne Zookes' life hung in the balance. He would see to her immediate care and deliver her safely to the hospital. The paramedics placed her on a stretcher and loaded her into the light green Freightliner Medic Master emergency vehicle. Big Bob's radio unsquelched as the Trauma Center's head surgeon discussed Bob's findings of the young woman's condition.

During the transport, Big Bob's assistant, Lois, provided him with an overview of the woman's emergency information. Lois had retrieved this information from the publishing firm's human resource manager whom she met at the scene while the other paramedics performed their tasks. He read the clipboard notes. They stated her name as Delores Anne Zookes, nicknamed Daisy. She had light brown hair and blue eyes. He read further to find her age listed at twenty-eight and her marital status marked single. She had been employed as a professional writer for the Hannah and Rhutkers JC Publishing Company for approximately five years. Her height and weight were average; she stood five feet four inches tall and weighed one hundred and twenty-four pounds. With no known allergies to medications or food, her blood type was listed as A negative. He noticed her address placed her not too far from the Benson Building in an apartment on upper Fifth Avenue. Big Bob double-checked the paperwork and handed the clipboard back to Lois. This information would be supplied to the front desk at the Trauma Center. He continued overseeing the care of Daisy during her transport.

Chapter Four:

THE OPPORTUNITY

Daisy came upon a road made of solid stone, devoid of painted lines and street signs. Turning left for lack of direction, she started walking the road. Within minutes she heard the clip clop of a horse approaching from behind. She waited by the side of the road as a horse –white with black flecks covering its fur – pulling a carriage came to a halt alongside her. The driver of the carriage tipped his hat and smiled. He wore an old-fashioned dark-colored suit and donned a brown hat. A white, ruffled shirt protruded out of his breast jacket and sleeves.

With a warm and reassuring smile he asked, "Are you in need of a lift?"

Daisy stood gaping without answering.

The driver asked again, "I say, Miss, would you be in need of a lift somewhere?"

Just then three tiny heads poked out from the carriage side window - two boys about the ages of nine and ten and a sweet little girl of about age seven. They were giggling and staring at Daisy. A woman's voice instructed the children to stop staring.

"Why yes, I could use a ride to somewhere," stammered Daisy to the kind driver.

He nodded his head and the door to the carriage opened. Daisy joined the foursome in the carriage. Without delay the horse started trotting onward in the same direction. She imagined one would be jostled about when riding in a horse and buggy, but this carriage seemed to glide on air.

The woman accompanying the three children wore a two-piece, light blue tailored dress, a design from around the turn of the twentieth century. Her outfit matched the driver's as far as time period. She had brunette hair done in a style befitting the outfit, with an elegant hat that complemented the dress. She wore white gloves and sported laced boots. The boys wore white shirts, light gray knickers with suspenders, knee high socks and brown shoes; the young girl wore a frilly white blouse, a pretty blue ankle length skirt and black shiny shoes with bows. They were a happy bunch as one could see.

Inside the spacious carriage, light tan leather adorned the walls and upholstery. Velvety cloth cushions made the firm seating cozier. The opened windows allowed a soft breeze to flow into the spacious sitting area. The children played simple games with each other and said please and thank you whenever they weren't giggling.

"Welcome to the Province of Niv," said the woman.

Daisy turned to face the women while trying to ascertain what she had just said.

Noticing Daisy's bewildered expression the woman repeated her greeting and extended her hand, "I said welcome to Niv. I believe this is your first time here."

"Umm, yes. I guess it is?" stammered Daisy as they shook hands. "Where did you say we are? I'm all mixed up at the moment and I'm not sure of my whereabouts. In fact, I think I'm lost. The only sign I have seen thus far has been at Mirror Lake. I'm not sure how I came to be there. Sorry if this isn't making any sense."

Never taking her eyes from Daisy, the woman answered, "You are in the province of Niv. We have visitors passing through here all the time. People come and people go, each one getting an opportunity to decide if this is the place they would one day hope to call home. If you plan to continue your journey through the province then I'd say that you are in for a great adventure. By the way, my name is Veronica, Veronica Heartsworth. My friends call me Roni. These three giggling children are Chancy, Chi, and Candrise." The boys each shook Daisy's hand and the little girl curtsied.

"My name is Delores Anne Zookes. My friends call me

Daisy. Did you say the province of Niv? I've never heard of it or seen it on a map." Flustered, she continued, "It appears that I might have interrupted a stagecoach scene on a movie set. Pardon me if I interrupted your shoot. I shouldn't have been walking in the area of your cast and set. I do like the look of your costumes and this carriage."

Reassuring Daisy that she hadn't interrupted anything Roni said, "The children and I are out for a joy ride. We were looking forward to meeting you."

Roni's statement perplexed Daisy causing her to say, "I don't quite understand. I am from Indiana. I am supposed to be at work and I need to get back there. My boss expects me to finish an adventure story within six more weeks. You see, I am a writer for a publishing firm and..." Daisy stopped mid-sentence, realizing her rattling on made little sense. In her nervousness, she became quiet and looked at the four faces studying her.

Roni smiled as she said, "Nice to meet you Delores Anne Zookes—Daisy. I like that name Daisy. I do hope it is all right if I call you Daisy, for I feel as though we were friends at heart straight away. Do please call me Roni. And no, you did not interrupt a TV shoot or anything like that. Most visitors are a bit baffled when they first arrive in Niv. Once the journey begins, they don't have much time to worry about those other things. You will be able to put your mind at rest as you encounter all the sights and wonders of Niv. It's only natural that you have questions." Roni put a hand on Daisy's knee and gave it a tender pat. She continued, "I can see that you want answers and are eager to start. I hope the children aren't disturbing you?"

Daisy turned her attention back to the children who stared at her as if she were the one wearing an outlandish costume.

Roni went on, "The province of Niv has been around a very long time. It has a beautiful countryside with plenty of vegetation, streams, animals, and cozy cottages. The main city is located down the road a ways on the far north side of the province. This place offers much to see and do."

"So much to see and do here? Why I haven't seen anything except Mirror Lake, one sign, and the road we are traveling on. Are we talking about the same place?"

Roni encouraged Daisy to look out her window and to see the animated life taking place in the province of Niv. Daisy strained her eyes as she looked out the carriage window and viewed the same thing she had earlier; namely, rolling fields of green grass and some mountains off in the distance. Since they had long passed the lake, she couldn't even see that anymore.

"I don't see anything alive or animated taking place here," said Daisy.

Roni squeezed Daisy's knee and encouraged her to look again as they overheard the children's giggling.

As Daisy turned to look again, she couldn't believe all that she saw. The whole place came to life right outside the carriage window. People with children strolled about amongst a variety of cottages. Animals and farmers were working on their farms, and others frolicked in open meadows. People riding bicycles came into view. She saw magnificent trees, bushes, shrubs and flowers all in full bloom. Casting her gaze out the other side of the carriage, streams and fountains overflowing came into view. More homes with quaint paths leading up to them were outlined with multiple species of flowers. People were active. A combination of young and old, male and female tended the homes, farms, and fields. Various farm animals could be seen grazing in the near and far fields without fences. Then she saw flocks of birds flying in a range of formations across the cloudless sky. Off in the distance appeared larger buildings, representative of a city. The scene developed as she looked on. It appeared as though she were in a darkroom watching the process of a developing picture come to life.

Roni continued, "Niv has a great deal to offer, with much to see and experience. Please don't be too hasty to leave. I am sure you will find your way."

Daisy leaned back and continued to view the scene. As she studied the children, Roni, and the carriage, she realized that she was someplace outside her normal realm of life. She had a sense of peace and calm as her feminine intuition assured her this was a safe place. Her temples began to ache as she tried to remember what had happened to her before waking up at the lake. She thought that perhaps she had been driving her car and had been in an accident. She reasoned this could be the afterlife or whatever one calls it. A solemn feeling washed over her knowing she had somehow left Indianapolis. This prompted her to ask Roni, "How did you and the children come to be in Niv? Have you lived here very long?'

"The children and I live in a cottage over the hillside in the city of Niv. It is a lovely home that the Prince of Niv prepared for us. We came here years ago when my husband abandoned us on the Oregon Trail. His name was Howard Heartsworth. He came from a wealthy, fine, upstanding Massachusetts family. His butler, Franklin Floydd Knight, who is now driving the carriage, accompanied us on the Oregon Trail. Howard meant well, but he had a gambling problem. Through his own foolish schemes, he lost his entire inheritance. Hoping to find a better life, we headed west to a new frontier. But once the gold strike news reached our group of weary travelers, Howard became obsessed with the idea this could be his chance to make things right. Franklin, even though he worked for Howard, stayed back with the children and me as he thought it unthinkable to abandon us on the Trail. Howard left with some rowdy men in search of gold with a promise that he would be back just as soon as he could. After his departure our entire wagon party encountered a severe snowstorm along the Trail. About two weeks later, a hunting party trapping furs came upon our camp. They

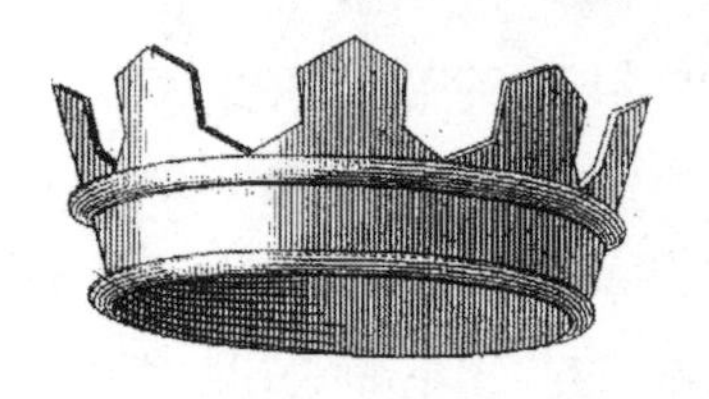

found the children embraced by my frozen body and all the others frozen and huddled together in small groups under snow-covered blankets. The children and I are now citizens of Niv who live in the great city's center. The King of Niv, who is also the Prince, has provided for the children and I more than we could have ever hoped or dreamed. I think it would be a joy for you to meet him. He is ever so gracious and takes time out for everyone who gets a chance to visit. He'd be a good one to ask for help and directions. Surely, he will help you out with your needs and circumstances. The Prince himself sent us out today in search of you."

Daisy sat back absorbing all that Roni had told her. She found this information disturbing, causing her to question if she wanted to know more about this place. Still, she wanted to figure out how to get back to Indianapolis and to her work. Perplexed, her mind raced as she questioned how she ever wound up in a carriage with a nice woman named Roni and her three children learning about this place called Niv. Contemplative, she wondered if she should answer Roni's beckoning assertion to go and meet this King or Prince of Niv?

Roni interrupted her thoughts, "Go meet him Daisy. He will tell you what you need to know, and then you will be on your way. You could hear what his plans are and learn about becoming a citizen of the province. What do you have to lose?"

Roni spoke again, "One sees things more clearly here in Niv. If you like adventures, as the children and I do, then you would enjoy a tour around Niv. It's your choice as no one else can make it for you."

Daisy could sense that Roni had given her some kind of an ultimatum. At that, Daisy looked out the window and thought for a moment, "Mmmph, the province of Niv, and an adventure. Well what could it hurt? I am in need of some material for that story Strain is expecting from me. I could explore this place for a while. Maybe Roni will let me use her phone once we get to her house. I could call and let someone back home know where I am. According to my feminine radar, it seems pretty safe here. Plus Roni's children don't seem as they would be too much hassle or bother to hang around with for a while. I'll tell Roni it's a deal."

Daisy had just about answered Roni with a yes, when Roni tapped Daisy's knee and said, "Great! It's settled then."

Daisy's eyes popped with stupefaction as to how Roni knew she had decided to stay and tour through the province of Niv. Plus, she still didn't know the general location of Niv. Daisy felt a sudden panic attack coming on as she realized the ramifications of her decision. She swallowed hard and fought against the feelings of panic.

Right then the carriage came to a complete stop as she heard the driver call out, "Whoa."

With gentle kindness, Roni grasped Daisy by the two hands

and said, "I am so happy for your decision." Then she chattered on some more about the goodness and graciousness of the King and how meeting him would be good for Daisy.

Then Roni said, "Perhaps, I have said too much already and have your head spinning with information. You could still change your mind, but I do hope you will stay. All I can say is to make your way to the city and that's where the King will be."

Daisy remained caught up in what Roni had said. The stagecoach door opened. With apprehension, Daisy took this as her cue to exit. Roni leaned toward Daisy, touching her knee saying, "We will have to say goodbye for now."

"But," faltered Daisy as she made a methodical movement to disembark from the carriage. Once her feet were planted on the road she turned to face them. Roni, the children, and the driver looked at her with expectant expressions on their faces. She asked Roni, "How will I know the way, and what am I supposed to do?"

Roni called to her as the carriage starting moving, "Make up your mind at the gate if you want to go back to where you were or if you want to follow the road further into Niv and have the adventure of your life. The choice is yours and yours alone. Au revoir, my new friend Daisy." At that the carriage took off and the children waved and yelled goodbye.

"Goodbye," called Daisy as she stood waving and watching till the carriage traveled from her sight.

Chapter Five:

THE DIAGNOSIS

The paramedics delivered Daisy to the Indianapolis Trauma Center's emergency room where a medical team took over her care. The medical staff hovered around Daisy's unconscious body, analyzing her condition. The sustained sizable skull fracture that rendered her unconscious garnered their chief concern. The deep gaping wound to this area had been clamped shut by the paramedics to control the bleeding. It would require stitches. The lower half of her left leg had doubled in size due to swelling caused by multiple sprains. The bruising of her right collarbone along with some cracked ribs affected her breathing. She had broken two fingers on her right hand and her left wrist was swollen and blue. She displayed symptoms of shock due to the various broken bones, and her blood pressure dropped below normal. She remained unconscious as the trauma team continued their examination and began running various tests.

They utilized the Glasgow coma scale to rate her coma.

The test results from this scale would provide a scoring range enabling the neurosurgeons to judge the severity of her coma. The scores would stem from a battery of tests in conjunction with the eye opening, motor responses, and verbal responses. The neurosurgeons' findings would be calculated with a possible range of scores from three to fifteen points. The lower the score on the Glasgow coma scale, the more severe the coma.

Daisy began to show signs of swelling within her cranial region due to the skull fracture and internal bleeding. The doctor ordered a CAT scan and an MRI done to determine the degree of injuries. He also ordered a full body scan to see if she had any other areas of internal bleeding or hemorrhaging. Once she was stabilized, the medical staff transported her for the various testing and scans.

Per notification of next of kin, the trauma center telephoned Daisy's parents, Mr. and Mrs. Jonathan J. Zookers. When Dr. Wilfred Kabintzol, the overseeing physician of Daisy's care could break away, he spoke with her parents on the telephone. He gave a brief explanation of the treatment performed on their daughter thus far. Since her parents lived in Pennsylvania, he suggested it might be in their best interest to come to their daughter's aide. Dr. Kabintzol had a family of his own and could hear the concern in the Zookers' stricken voices. He answered their many questions and reassured them the medical team would continue to do all they could for their daughter's injuries.

When Dr. Kabintzol returned to the emergency trauma room, the medical team informed him that they had determined that Daisy had hit her head first.

An assistant said, "Hitting her head first would have rendered her unconscious after the first impact. Then she must have continued her fall down the staircase judging by the various types and placements of her bruises and injuries."

Dr. Kabintzol interjected, "That would explain the unusual bruising all over her body. It's obvious she did not shield herself from further injury during her fall. The blunt force trauma to her skull pictured on the MRI shows the cranial region received the initial full impact of her fall."

Another member of the team asked, "Doctor, how long do you think, before she regains consciousness?"

"The Glasgow coma scale results have rated the patient's score in the region between twelve and thirteen. This indicates the coma to be borderlining a mild to moderate comatose case. However, due to her other multiple injuries, her body's response to treatment could prolong her recovery and impact how long she will remain comatose. The neurosurgeon has decided that a short procedure surgery should be performed to reduce the fluid buildup culminating from the skull fracture. The patient is being prepped for surgery as we speak. We are hopeful that there hasn't been any crucial damage to the brain. We will need to keep any excessive pressure from developing within the cranial area."

The assistant added, "Right now, the coma is working in the patient's favor then, since it is imperative to have little or no movement of the patient's head at this present time of her condition."

"As long as we keep the swelling down in the cranial area," the doctor said, "we should reduce the risk of her entering into a long-term coma."

The team had to disperse at these words. Some had to go into surgery and the others were being paged for another new arrival. Another busy day as the Indianapolis Trauma Center moved into high gear.

An anxious young man sat in the emergency room waiting area hoping to hear any word about Daisy's condition or some news of the various tests and procedures being conducted. Paul had briefly spoken with a receptionist at the emergency room check-in desk asking about Delores Zookes's condition. However, because his name didn't appear on Ms. Zookes's emergency medical information card as a point of contact, they were prohibited from providing him any information concerning her health.

Darla Mae had called Paul from her cell phone as soon as she had learned the specifics about Daisy's accident. Darla knew that Paul would want to know. Of all the men her friend Daisy had dated, Darla favored Paul. She never mentioned this to Daisy, as she hoped her friend would some day see the light and end up with Paul.

Paul Thornchen drove straight away to the hospital. He had asked Darla several questions. She filled him in on all she knew concerning Daisy's condition. Paul had made up his mind on the way to the hospital that he would stay at Daisy's side. He telephoned his place of employment and put in for a short leave of absence. If Daisy's injuries were as bad as Darla had explained to him on the telephone then she would be in the hospital for some time. Being on good terms with his boss made this decision easier.

Paul had been in love with Daisy since the first time he met her at the house of one of his friends. She had stopped by with one of her girlfriends who happened to be dating Paul's friend. Paul and his friend were watching a football game when the two girls stopped in to say hello. In an instant, Paul knew he would like to go out with Daisy. He liked her fresh, warm smile and her energetic, upbeat conversation. Best of all, Paul thought she had dreamy blue eyes. From that day forward, he would set up dates with Daisy from time to time. He wanted to see if she would fall for him as he had for her. Paul did not shove his intentions onto Daisy, even though he felt that one day he would like to marry her. He respected her too much to be pushy or demanding. He kept hoping. Now that she needed him, he would go to her. Putting on the male armor of protector and confidant suited him well. Paul knew that Daisy thought his slow lane approach to life was a sign of weakness. Yet, he did not feel this way. He deemed it important to have strength of character and to be patient in dealing with others. Those who were close to Paul knew him to be strong in character and knew he possessed firmness within his good nature. His father taught and showed him that a man made of steel does not easily bend.

Paul would wait at the trauma center until someone could give him some information concerning Daisy's care, or he'd wait until he could go in and see her. In the meantime, he would pray for her.

Chapter Six:

BEGIN AGAIN THOROUGHFARE

With the carriage out of sight, Daisy remained standing at a T-intersection. A memorized portion of a verse she had learned during childhood shot through her mind, "For I know the plans I have for you." She surmised if she ever needed a plan of action, she needed one now. It bothered her that Roni had dropped her off as she had just begun to get a grip on her bearings. Now, the first people she met have left her without a map, without money, and without even the hope of a telephone call home. Her thoughts turned to the interesting conversation with Roni in the carriage. At least she knew the name of the place, which she said aloud, "The province of Niv."

Daisy made a mental note of the direction the carriage traveled. To her left the road led to a cut, stone wall with a tall wooden arched gate propped wide open. These words were etched onto a rough piece of lumber above the arched opening: "Back to Where You Were."

Daisy stood with her hands on her hips as she read the words and voiced a simple, "Huh!"

She turned, facing the direction the carriage had traveled. Daisy figured that direction would lead into the city and take her on some type of an adventure. Roni had told her going into the city would provide a chance to meet with some King or Prince of Niv.

Again, out of nowhere appeared a street name at the T – intersection: "Begin Again Thoroughfare." Daisy thought it a peculiar name for a road.

She needed to make a decision. Should she go straight through the gate that might lead her back, or should she head in the direction of the carriage adventuring onto Begin Again Thoroughfare?

"Go back, Go back," echoed a voice she thought came from her subconscious. Daisy didn't see the figure hiding behind the gate chiding in a low voice for her to go through the gate. As she began to make her way towards the open gate, a hoard of brown and orange butterflies flew around her. They engulfed and encased her within their fluttering wings.

They were beautiful, delicate creatures, as butterflies tended to be. She flung her arms about swooshing them away, being careful not to harm them. She heard laughter coming from a tree branch overhead as she shoed away the butterflies. Startled, she turned and looked up to see an owl perched on a branch, laughing with a human-like voice.

SPOTTY

Caught off guard, she yelled, "Yikes, it's an owl laughing at me." She became frightened and went to take off running.

But the owl laughed again and said, "Oh, don't be afraid, I won't hurt you. I enjoyed watching your encounter with the butterflies."

Daisy stopped in her tracks and turned to face the owl saying, "But you're an owl. Owls aren't supposed to talk or laugh."

"But you were so funny to watch, I couldn't help but laugh. I am glad you were ever so gentle with those delicate Oregon Silverspot Butterflies."

"The what?" replied Daisy.

"The Oregon Silverspot Butterflies, the ones you were shooing away. They are from the coastal meadows located in the Pacific Northwest of the United States. They are a threatened butterfly species due to a loss of habitat, along with the decline of its host plant called the Early Blue Violet," explained the owl.

"Oh, I see," said Daisy. She didn't see or understand what the owl said, and she didn't know enough about endangered species to question him either. Plus, she had no desire to process any endangered species information or to speak with an owl either. She wanted to be on her way.

The owl asked, "Don't you care?"

"Care? Care about what?" asked Daisy with a confused look on her face. "Hey, wait a minute. This is weird talking to an owl. Why owls aren't suppose to speak," muttered Daisy more to herself than to the owl.

"Everything and everyone has permission to speak within the province of Niv," said the owl. "Furthermore, in the province we care and are concerned about one another. Did you know that the Oregon Silverspot Butterfly is an endangered species, Ms. Uh, what did you say your name was?" questioned the owl.

"I didn't say," responded Daisy with her arms crossed.

Realizing that he had upset her, the owl softened his next words, "Please forgive me; I think we got off to a bad start. By the way, my name is Spotty. I am sorry if I offended you. It's just that I am so passionate about all my dear friends who are endangered or who are threatened that sometimes I get carried away with my zealousness for their welfare."

Seeing the owl's concern for the butterflies and his sorrow for upsetting her, Daisy too softened her reply and dropped her defensive stature, "My name is Delores Anne Zookes, but my friends call me Daisy." With her introduction complete,

she studied the owl and saw that he had large black eyes encircled with radiating light brown feathers. He had a curved tan beak, a belly covered with white feathers and horizontal brown bars of feathers. His wings were thick with brown feathers with white bars. He bore sharp talons on his toes.

"Well it's very nice to meet you Miss Daisy," said Spotty. "What did you think of the butterflies?"

"I thought that the butterflies were, well, umm, butterflies. Did you say they were in danger or something?" questioned Daisy.

"Yes I did. You see many of the creatures within the Province are here due to extinction or the possibility of extinction; several are on the endangered species listing. Do you know what endangered means?" asked Spotty.

Daisy didn't hesitate to answer, "Of course I do. It means being in danger of extermination or dying out." Daisy took great pride in the fact that she had excelled in her education. Her continuing education at the Writer's College had paid off for her young professional career.

They were quiet for a few seconds then Daisy asked, "Spotty are you on the endangered species list?"

Glad she took an interest, Spotty sat more erect and answered, "Yes, I am. I am a Northern Spotted Owl. My feathered spotted friends and I are in danger of becoming extinct. My species once lived in the dense, old-growth forests in the Pacific Northwest of the United States and Canada; but we had to leave because of a loss of our habitat. Upon my arrival into Niv, it has been my duty to inform others about all the different species that are endangered, and to report my findings back to the King of Niv."

"Oh," said Daisy, "that seems like quite a big undertaking."

"Yes it is. Some think I am a wise old owl. But the truth is that any wisdom I have for doing my job comes from all that I have learned in Niv. In the province of Niv resides a home for wisdom, and I do feel right at home here," Spotty said.

After another pause of silence Spotty asked, "Are you concerned about becoming extinct?"

With a bewildered look, Daisy said, "Extinction at my age? I'm only twenty-eight years old. My grandmother and grandfather lived well into their late nineties. You know Spotty after all this talk about wisdom that seems like a silly question."

Spotty didn't respond, but he cocked his head looking at her with raised eyebrows.

Daisy surveyed her surroundings and sat down. She criss-crossed her legs and rested her chin into the palm of her hand saying, "What am I to do? I don't know how I got here, and my head starts throbbing every time I try to think too much. This entire day has left me feeling weary. And now I find myself talking to an owl." At this she started to cry - a good long cry. She needed to let go of all the angst of the day. Spotty waited until she had composed herself before making a suggestion.

After a good seven minutes or so Spotty asked in a serious tone, "What is it you want to do at this very moment in your life Daisy?"

Sniffling, Daisy considered her options and said, "If truth be told, I'm not sure. I think I should find my way back. On the other hand, I am becoming more curious about the direction my new friend Roni traveled. She had mentioned a city and a King."

"Say, I have an idea," brightened Spotty. "I have to go into the city and provide my updated six-month endangered species report to the King. You could accompany me. Since I know my way around the province, I could act as your tour guide to the city." Spotty had the habit of being an old chatterbox and he hoped to fill her in on the many threatened and endangered species contained in his research. Then he added, "Plus if you would like to meet with the King, perhaps I could arrange it on the day that I meet with him. What do you think, Daisy?"

Daisy viewed her new-feathered friend with her eyebrows slanted in towards her nose. Reminding her of Strain looming about their work cubicles, this caused her to chuckle. She told Spotty, "This journey could provide the material I need for the Adolescents-do-Read Publication's adventure story that I am working on for my boss." She then proceeded to fill Spotty in on this recent project at work and her dilemma and negligence in putting together the adventure story.

"Surely, with a talking owl and a ride in a horse-drawn carriage already under your belt, more ideas could come your way on the road called Begin Again Thoroughfare. After all, what do you have to lose if you spend a day or two away from the office?"

Daisy reasoned once she had gathered enough adventure material, she could follow the road returning to this large opened gate and go back. It sounded strange even as she thought it through, but this whole day had been out of the ordinary. She surprised herself with how she had begun to adjust and to accept her unusual circumstances.

With a premature confidence in Spotty she said to him, "I trust that you will be a knowledgeable tour guide; and later, you can help me find my way back with plenty of adventure material tucked away for my story."

"It's a deal."

She nodded her head toward Spotty, pleased at having made a decision. Also, she prided herself at being a seasoned traveler and a well-read woman of the world. Lost in thought she rationalized that while embarking on this journey, she would help Spotty in his quest for his endangered friends. She did have some knowledge and awareness about the plight of endangered species with man and the ever-changing environment. She suggested to Spotty, "Maybe the King of Niv could provide some insight and help to devise a plan for the problem. After all, you had mentioned you would be bringing the King an updated extinction report."

"Well now, let's take it one step at a time and get to the city of Niv first. We can discuss these issues along the way."

Daisy agreed.

This thought probed Spotty's heart; "embarking on this journey could open the door to Daisy about the most significant endangered plan in the works. It could reveal the species the King of Niv holds nearest and dearest to his heart. The main species, which remains in serious jeopardy of becoming extinct."

Daisy stretched and yawned and said to Spotty, "It's a deal."

"Good," said Spotty, "but first we better find some lodging as it is getting late and you appear to need some rest. You do seem a bit tired."

"I am," said Daisy.

They started their journey on Begin Again Thoroughfare and happened upon a house close by. A small realtor's container hooked to a post signified a house for sale. An "Open House" sign hung in the front window of the house.

Daisy made her way to the post and reached into the bin, pulling out a pamphlet. The header read, Wisdom Real-Estate with a picture of the house on the pamphlet. Underneath the picture, the agent posted the house's address: 001 Begin Again Thoroughfare, Province of Niv, in the State of GN, ZIP-CODE 137731. The real estate agent's advertisement announced a special: "One free-night stay to the reader of this pamphlet."

Daisy read the pamphlet aloud and Spotty said, "Well then this is the place. You go in and make yourself comfortable. I'll sleep out here on this tree branch next to the front porch. I'm sure you'll find everything you need inside."

Too tired to argue or to question, she went inside the house. She found everything she needed inside the furnished little home. She didn't reach for a light switch because daylight still poured in through the windows. She'd decided to question Spotty in the morning about the nighttime still remaining light as though it were mid-day. Along with other things, this didn't make any sense to her. She entered the kitchen area and saw a bowl set up with free flowing water draining into a larger oval container. She used the water to freshen up and to take a drink. A table and a chair stood in the kitchen. A pink notebook with a yellow number-two pencil lay on the table. When she picked up the pencil, she had a déjà vu moment.

Back at the hospital her heart monitor began registering a sudden rise in Daisy's heart rate. The medical attendant came into her room to check the erratic beeping of the pulse machine.

Glad for the pink notebook, she decided to use it to journal her time in Niv. Daisy relished knowing she could take tangible notes for the adventure story. This made the task of writing a story less daunting. Prior to being commissioned for this project, the stories she had written had been about real people and real places. Fiction had not been her forte. Strain stayed oblivious to this fact, as he had quizzed her about this minor difficulty for creating the adventure story for the adolescent publication series; meanwhile, he remained clueless to these facts.

Daisy began penciling in the notebook a list of stories she had previously written. Her two main reasons for moving from Pennsylvania to Indianapolis were a college scholarship and her great interest in the lifestyle of the Indianapolis 500 Speedway racecar drivers. She interviewed and published personal adventure stories about the life and excitement of various Indy racecar drivers. She learned that racecar drivers were risk takers on and off the racetrack.

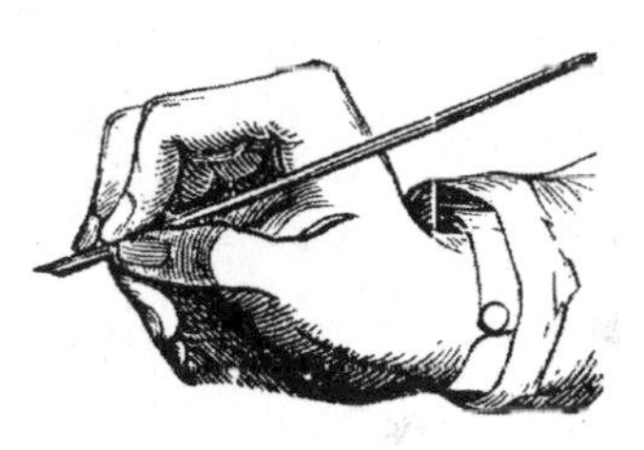

The second story she put on the list took place last fall. She had interviewed a team of four nature explorers who completed an eight-week hiking expedition traversing the Rocky Mountains. While she did not go there herself, she utilized the four nature explorers' journals and captivated the readers with their awesome photographs captioning majestic scenes.

Then she listed an article she had written detailing Texan families who have endured hardships living in the Galveston area. The article detailed the never-ending coastal storms, which ravage their homes and livelihood off the Gulf of Mexico.

Last on the list, she wrote down her most recent venture to an isolated island near upper Michigan with an offshore drilling expedition. Assigned as the official note taker, she had been invited to accompany a group of environmentalists. From her notes, she created a successful piece for an elite-drilling magazine.

Sitting at the small kitchen table, she continued to write all that had transpired since she had awakened at Mirror Lake. Daisy fell asleep in the chair at the table.

Chapter Seven:

TULIP

Tulip received a telephone call from her mother notifying her of Daisy's accident. Her mother relayed everything the doctor had said concerning Tulip's sister's condition. With her husband's assistance and encouragement, Tulip contacted the airlines and caught the first available flight to Indianapolis. Because of tightened airport security, Tulip made sure to carry two forms of identification bearing her full name - Teressa Lee Zookers Cavenei.

Tulip studied her driver's license photo noting she could still pass as Daisy's twin. Only one year older than Daisy, she had the more serious nature of the two siblings.

Tulip resided in the mid-sized town of Uppercrest, Pennsylvania close to her parents. She had married her high school sweetheart and they had two boys. Aside from being an accomplished pianist, she had social graces epitomizing femininity. But when it came to her husband and their two boys, she could camp and fish with the best of them. Being a devout Christian woman, she always mentioned her sister during prayer time.

Before leaving for the airport, she and her husband said a quick prayer for her parents' safety. They were driving to Indianapolis since their father disliked flying on airplanes. Tulip cried her heart out while sitting on the plane as it taxied onto the runway. She could only think of Daisy, her best friend and sister.

Tulip had made hotel arrangements for her and her parents near the trauma center. They preferred this to staying at Daisy's one-bedroom apartment located across town. Upon landing, Tulip took a cab from the airport to the hotel. She asked the cabbie to wait while taking care of their room accommodations. She placed her bags in her suite and peeked in on the adjoining suite for her parents. Once she had checked in, the cabbie drove her to the trauma center.

Her heavy heart lifted when she saw Paul in the waiting room. She found it comforting to have someone with her upon seeing Daisy in the emergency room. After initial greetings, Paul and she went straight away to Daisy's bedside.

Tulip had met Paul on a prior visit and found his attitude and outlook refreshing. She favored him over all the fellows Daisy had thus far introduced to her.

Upon seeing the contusion to Daisy's forehead, both Paul and Tulip had to fend off their tears of dread. She appeared to be resting, but it became apparent that she had suffered multiple injuries. Grief stricken, Tulip leaned into Paul's chest and wept.

A nurse paged Dr. Kabintzol; and he made his way to Daisy's room. After introductions the doctor said, "I am glad you were able to find an afternoon flight Mrs. Cavenei. I can see that you are tired and anxious, so I will keep it brief. Your sister's cranial fracture has put her into a coma. All indications show that when she fell in the stairwell she hit her head first. Then she proceeded to tumble like a rag doll down the stairwell where she sustained all her other injuries."

Tulip gasped as she pictured Daisy falling as the doctor described, and Paul took hold of her arm to steady her.

The doctor continued, "This serious blow to the head cracked her skull. We preformed a short procedure to keep the fluid from building up around the brain."

Tulip asked, "How long will she be in a coma?"

"The neurosurgeon rated the coma between twelve and thirteen, which indicates a moderate comatose case. However, with all the other injuries putting a strain onto her weakened system, this will affect and determine how long she remains in a coma."

The doctor proceeded to show and explain her bruises, broken bones, and sprains. The main focus of concern remained the skull fracture.

Paul and Tulip continued to question the doctor about every procedure they had performed on Daisy, including the medication flowing from an intravenous drip bag next to her bed.

Tulip explained that her mother and father would be arriving later that night, as Dr. Kabintzol wanted to confer with them as well. Receiving a page, he provided them with his contact information and left the room.

A receptionist entered the room to discuss some paperwork concerns with Tulip.

She asked, "Could you please provide the correct spelling of Delores's last name. The emergency contact information supplied by her employer listed the family's name as Zookers and her name as Zookes. It appears to be a typo."

"My sister Daisy changed her last name from Zookers to Zookes upon being hired as a professional writer. We both had endured teasing from classmates during our Pymatuning, Pennsylvania school years due to our last name. My sister thought Zookes sounded more professional, so she had it changed. Zookers is the correct spelling of our parents' last name for the emergency contact information."

The receptionist thanked Tulip and gave her condolences to both of them before exiting the room. Before leaving the room she did mention about the trauma center's cafeteria remaining open twenty-four hours.

Paul and Tulip decided to get a cup of coffee and headed to the cafeteria. Neither wanted to leave Daisy's side, but both were exhausted and in need of some sustenance. They ran into Darla at the elevator, who preferred to see Daisy first but consented to join them for coffee. Without a family member present, Darla knew she would be prohibited entrance to the emergency area.

Along with Paul, Tulip had previously met Darla on her few visits to Indianapolis. With coffee in hand, the threesome sat down, updating Darla on what the doctor had said concerning Daisy's condition.

Darla shared how the office cubicles were all abuzz with many different versions of how Daisy fell in the stairwell.

"One person even claimed that a mystery person had shoved her while stealing her purse. Yes, the rumor mill is alive and well at the Benson Building. Strain kept pacing about with his eyebrows bent in towards his nose ordering everyone to get back to work. It has been a crazy day at work."

The three caught up on small talk while drinking another cup of coffee and munching on a sandwich. It had been a while since the last time they were together.

Tulip reminisced about how excited Daisy had been when she left for Indianapolis years ago. "My sister made up her mind upon high school graduation. Once she obtained a partial scholarship to attend the Indiana Writers Institute, she would move to Indianapolis and become a journalist. Even in high school, Daisy had a passion for writing. She told me she would major in journalism with a minor in literature. I remember the phone call I received from her mentioning how she had impressed her college professors with her writing flair. This is what prompted them to introduce her to the editor-in-chief of the Hannah and Rhutkers JC Publishing Company; and thus began Daisy's publishing career during her junior year of college. She has worked full-time and often over-time, all the while continuing her educational goals of obtaining a bachelor of science degree before she turns thirty. It's difficult to keep up with her energetic personality."

Paul smiled and said, "She is a remarkable woman. I sometimes feel one has to run to stay abreast of her."

"Well, she is good at what she does," added Darla. "I hear among our fellow workers how they brag about her work. She enjoys writing, that's for sure."

Once they finished their sandwiches, they went back to the emergency room to keep a vigil at Daisy's bedside. They spoke to Daisy and prayed she would wake up. A bond of understanding and trust began to form among these three individuals.

Now even more grateful to have Darla with them, Tulip's mind wandered to her parents driving from Pennsylvania. They should be arriving within a few more hours.

Paul took time with Darla showing and explaining Daisy's medications and wounds.

Chapter Eight:

SIDETRACKED

After what seemed to be a several-hour rest, Daisy lifted her head from the kitchen table. The yellow number-two pencil had left an indentation on her right cheek, because she had fallen asleep while writing. Stretching and yawning, she saw a picture hanging over a fireplace in the adjoining room. Pictured close to volcanic slopes, a Hawaiian goose stood in some foliage. This goose is also known as a Nene. In the corner of the picture a short paragraph described the lush, tropical scene and the status of the small goose. It read, "The endangered Nene is the Hawaiian official state bird with about only eight hundred left in the wild." Saddened, Daisy shook her head. Remembering Spotty, she grabbed her notebook and the yellow number-two pencil and headed out the front door.

"Good morning," said Spotty, chuckling. "Did you rest well?"

The picture of the goose had disturbed her and put her in an unfriendly mood. "Fine," she uttered. "Could we get a move on? I'd like to start accumulating data to develop the adventure story and proceed on our mission towards the city of Niv."

"Boy, Miss Daisy, you sure don't waste any time once you make up your mind, do you?"

"I always like to jump-start my mornings and head early into work. If you can, tell me where I could find a bathroom; the house seems to be void of such a facility. I'd like to take care of myself and then we can begin our journey."

"Facilities? Bathroom? Why would you need to use a bathroom?"

Just then it dawned on Daisy that she hadn't needed a bathroom since waking up at Mirror Lake.

"Hey!" she replied, "What is up with that?"

Spotty explained how some of the bodily and health functions occur in the Province of Niv. He clarified, "Here, the body cleanses itself in another fashion. Once one consumes food or drink, the body breaks down the substance and evenly distributes it throughout the body. Any excess is turned into a gas caused by heat molecules within the body. This residual gas is emitted through the pours of the skin thereby eliminating any excess. In the province, we call this process skynthesis. And that, Ms. Daisy, is how one eliminates bodily waste in Niv."

Daisy stood amazed and dazed as she contemplated this information.

After his explanation of skynthesis he questioned, "Did you fail to notice that when you stood by certain trees their leaves would begin to shake, and that at other times certain blades of grass would turn in to your direction?"

"Yes, I did, but I had chalked that up to more peculiar happenings in this place called Niv. Therefore, I dismissed it. The leaves spooked me a little when they started shaking."

"When your body is emitting the gas—which is odorless—the grass and trees absorb it, using it for food. The gas emittal only occurs upon consumption of food or drink. Thus waste products don't exist in the province."

"You mean that no man or animal has to, you know, uh, go to the bathroom here in Niv?" uttered Daisy with disbelief.

"That's right. It's all taken care of utilizing the natural and effective process of skynthesis. However, once you leave the province, your body's functions will revert back to its, shall we say, normal conditional ways. By the way, are you hungry?"

At the mention of food, Daisy's eyes lit up.

"Good. Well then go back inside the house and get yourself some fruit and cheese. It should be sitting on the kitchen table and then we will be off."

Daisy hadn't noticed any food when she woke up with the yellow number-two pencil embedded onto her cheek. Obeying Spotty, she turned and went back inside the house. Sitting on the table sat a plate of cheeses and fruits, per Spotty's assertion. She ate her fill and took a drink of the basin's overflowing running water. She splashed some water onto her face and then dried off with a complimentary towel hanging on a wall rack.

Once back outside, the twosome started on their travels down Begin Again Thoroughfare. Daisy shared her frustration over the informative Hawaiian goose picture hanging over the fireplace in the small house. Spotty elaborated about the goose's habitat and mentioned his recent concern about its significant decline in numbers.

Since it was a nice clear day, Daisy enjoyed the walk and the conversation. When curiosity got the best of her, she asked the bird about the sun. She questioned him, "Is it morning or is it daytime? Where is the sun? I had noticed yesterday that the sky remained bright and beautiful all day, without a cloud in the sky. Can you explain this to me?"

"The city of Niv generates enough light and energy to supply the entire province. Therefore, it is unnecessary for the sun to yield its shine. A never-ending river runs its course through the province providing plenty of water, thus eliminating a need for rain clouds."

Spotty continued his dissertation about different operational features for plant life existence in Niv. He outlined a new dimension of photosynthesis and how it occurs due to the abundant supply of fresh oxygen, water, and light provided within the province. He explained in a scientific fashion about the energy source of light being supplied from the center of the City and how this affects the chlorophyll of the plants. These plants in turn derive their ongoing energy produced by the city's light source and mix with the emitted gases also caused during skynthesis.

This information had Daisy's head spinning and she made the comment, "This mind boggling explanation appears to be a plant life system in the form of a cylinder without a beginning or an end. One thing leads to and feeds into another."

"That is correct," said Spotty. "It is a self-sustaining, closed cycle system keeping all pollutants at bay, thus allowing no room for waste. Any and all outside pollutants would be unable to survive within the region."

Daisy asked if the moon and stars existed here. Spotty assured her that as they made their way into the great city she could visit the city's grand library where she could research material and data about the sky above, the atmospheric conditions, and the galaxies and stars. Her feathered friend said she would be quite pleased with her astronomical findings.

Spotty asked her, "Don't you find the blues skies blue enough?"

Daisy replied, "Oh they're deliciously blue. I feel like when I look up at the sky that I can almost touch the color blue itself." Daisy jotted all these notes and more into the pink notebook as they walked. She quoted in her notes, "The night never became dark. It resembled evening and then it became morning the following day. The vast enveloping blue canopy portrayed the sky, absent of the sun or moon."

Two deer made their way out of the thick shrubs and trees. They glanced at her and then at Spotty and then pranced away. She could hear children playing further up on one of the many paths protruding from the shady tree-lined road.

"The paths lead to several houses, similar to the one you stayed in last evening. Families or temporary house guests inhabit each house," said Spotty. "Our journey should take only about a day or two as it isn't a far distance to the city. It is imperative that we stick to the road."

He didn't clarify why they needed to stick to the road. Daisy understood by his matter-of-fact nature when he made the comment that perhaps something could happen if they ventured from Begin Again Thoroughfare.

While Daisy contemplated what Spotty had said, she heard the sound of a small-engine motorcycle coming up the thoroughfare. She waited along the side of the road as a young woman wearing a helmet pulled up on what looked like a yellow Vespa scooter. The girl turned off the engine and slipped off her helmet, greeting Daisy and Spotty. She wore her long red hair in a braid. Her blue jeans and jacket, accompanied by a yellow tee shirt suited her well. She had tennis shoes on her small feet, adding to her tomboyish appearance.

"Now Barbara this isn't the time for fun and games. We are on a mission into the City. I would appreciate it if you kept your visit short."

"Awe come on," said the girl named Barbara, "I enjoy meeting new people and having a little fun."

Daisy watched as Spotty and the girl—Barbara Charris—chided one another. When the girl turned toward Daisy, she grinned a big kid's smile and her smooth freckled complexion glowed.

After introductions Barbara asked Daisy if she would you like to go for a short ride down one of the paths.

"I just finished instructing her that we should to stick to the road," said Spotty.

"I'll have Daisy back in a jiffy," Barbara pleaded.

Spotty knew better than to give in. However, Barbara's sense of fun was contagious. Before he knew it, Daisy and Barbara were both donning helmets. The two girls sped off on the scooter down a path called Side Track. The tree-lined path led past cottages set far enough apart to accommodate gardens and open meadows. Small fenceless fields came into view at times with cows and sheep grazing.

Daisy clung to Barbara as they sped along on the motor scooter. The freckled, jean- clad girl seemed unworried that someone or something might venture in their way as they rounded a curve.

Barbara knew it was safe in the province. She enjoyed being a citizen of Niv. She loved riding all kinds of two-wheeled vehicles, even back in the day before Niv became her home. This new scooter of hers ran on clean air, and produced waste-free emissions. The exhaust system had some steam shooting out from time to time, as the tank had to be filled with water to keep the engine cool. She found it amazing what they could do with a little three-cylinder these days.

Growing up in San Francisco, Barbara had learned all about engines from her two brothers and her dad. Her mother always tried to get her to wear a dress, but Barbara wouldn't hear of it. She wanted to ride bikes and motorized vehicles; dresses weren't quite suited for this type of activity. In time, her mother relented and learned to appreciate Barbara's love for engines and two-wheeled contraptions.

In the province of Niv, Barbara delighted in giving newcomers a welcoming thrill ride on one of her scooters. Barbara and Daisy were making good headway until they came upon a brick someone had placed in the pathway and went flying into the bushes. Spotty had flown along, keeping them in view. He saw them wreck into the bushes with the small scooter.

Spotty knew something like this could happen. Spotty had lived in Niv long enough to know the works of the devious one called the Sly One. The Sly One did not live in the Province of Niv. On rare occasions the King granted him permission to enter the province. Spotty and the residents of Niv knew to keep their distance from the Sly One. They saw him for what he was and never gave him the time of day. However, visitors such as Daisy were naive about the Sly One and his tactics. Spotty discovered most visitors tended to underestimate the Sly One's trickery or the lengths to which he would go to scheme and mess up everyday life. Spotty knew for sure the Sly One had placed the brick on the path hoping to discourage and divert Daisy from their journey into the city.

Spotty spied a couple of neighbors who had heard the commotion. They came running from their homes to assist Daisy and Barbara. As a result of their spill, Daisy had scraped her knee causing her to limp a little. Determined to leave Niv with her notes when the time came, she had kept ahold of her pink notebook and the yellow number-two pencil. She had placed the notebook down her shirt and had put the pencil in her back pants pocket for safekeeping when she hopped onto the scooter. Barbara appeared to be banged up too, but remained her happy smiley self as they pulled themselves together. She always enjoyed life, and living in the province of Niv only added to that enjoyment.

Someone had pulled out a small cart from behind a house and urged Daisy and Barbara to hop in. Another person pushed Barbara's bike along side as they pulled the two girls in the cart to a local Wellness Station. Spotty flew overhead keeping watch on the crew, while Barbara and Daisy chatted away, laughing about their accident. Daisy liked Barbara and made mental notes to write down in her notebook all she had gleamed from her new scooter-riding friend.

"These people of Niv sure are kind and helpful. We didn't even have to ask them for assistance," said Daisy.

"People here see a need and they pitch right in and take

care of one another. "

Daisy found this comforting. As a stranger to Niv, this made her feel all the more secure in an unfamiliar place.

Chapter Nine:

THE ZOOKERS

Mr. and Mrs. Jonathan J. Zookers arrived later that evening after their eight-hour drive from Pennsylvania to Indianapolis. They met with Dr. Kabintzol as soon as they got to the hospital. He patiently re-explained most everything they had discussed about their daughter's injuries and care over their earlier telephone call. The doctor's fatherly instincts knew the importance of reinforcing and updating them on the health situation of their daughter. Daisy remained in a state of unconsciousness, unaware of the concerns being discussed so near to her.

The doctor spoke with confidence, reviewing all the professional medical procedures thus far performed. He reiterated the same details he had said to Tulip and Paul adding, "We have tended to and have treated all the breaks and bruises your daughter sustained in her fall. Even after your eight-hour journey, she still shows signs of shock. The medical staff will continue to keep a close watch for any internal bleeding or chance of infection. Now it will be a waiting game until she comes out of the coma. If you would like, you may keep a constant vigil at her bedside. In the past, we have found a more favorable prognosis with comatose patients who have had someone present, caring for them and speaking to them."

Jonathan thanked the doctor for his time and concern for his family's welfare, namely Daisy.

Once the doctor left, Tulip introduced Paul to her parents. Mr. Zookers eyed Paul and appreciated the man's firm handshake. He took an instant liking to this young man who was obviously fond of his daughter. Both Tulip and Paul volunteered to keep the vigil at Daisy's bedside.

Jonathan heard Tulip mention to her mother that Daisy's friend Darla had also been by, but she had left a few hours ago. He knew Martha would want to meet Darla and express her appreciation.

Jonathan and Martha Zookers were people strong in character, but seeing their daughter lying helpless on a hospital bed proved to be more than Martha could bear. Jonathan realized he would need to keep his wife somewhat distracted with the sights and sounds of the city. With Paul and Tulip assisting with the round-the clock-vigil, he would be able to spend time away from his daughter's bedside allowing his wife the time she needed to absorb the impact of the situation.

Later at their hotel, they met other folks who were assisting family members for medical reasons at the trauma center. Tulip's support and help proved an immense comfort. Martha would often gaze at Tulip, marveling at how much she and Daisy looked alike. Jonathan thought the world of his daughters and cherished every moment he could spend with them. He had been a good father, a kind and considerate man; but he had a firm hand when needed.

Jonathan spent the evening reminiscing about when they first began to operate the plant and tree nursery in Northeastern Pennsylvania. They called it the T & D Nursery after Daisy and Tulip. During the colder months they would sell autumn leaf sprigs and wreaths, gourds, Christmas trees, poinsettias, and various holiday wreaths. In the warmer months their greenhouses would come alive with every type of shrub and flower, plus any foliage they could fit or grow in their fields, greenhouses and work area. Being a botanist led him to nickname both of their daughters after flowers – Tulip and Daisy. Jonathan had a plaque on his office wall that read, "What You Feed Grows and What You Starve Dies." He had lived by this motto throughout his entire life. Acting as a caring parent, he showered his two girls with love, along

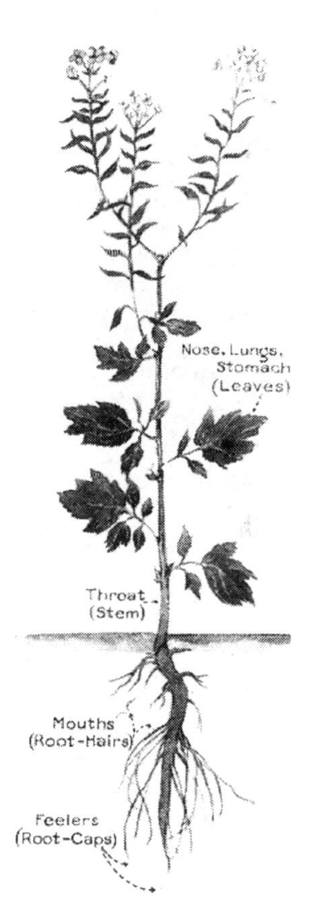

with teaching them responsibility, values, and understanding.

Toiling with a labor of love, he emphasized the sowing of seeds of peace within their neighborhood, among co-workers, and throughout their extended family. Now in the face of adversity and vulnerability, peace and love bloomed and radiated from his family's hearts. Mr. Zookers remained unaware of the positive effect his family's presence had on the hospital staff. The entire staff strove to be more sensitive and accommodating due to their sad and serious circumstances.

The doctor had told Jonathan that Daisy would be moved to a private room in the Intensive Care Unit. Jonathan's heart ached as he pictured the assortment of tubes stemming from his daughter's body providing medication, displaying her vital signs on monitors, and assisting with bodily functions. He knew his family would appreciate the private room. This would afford them privacy as they spoke endearing words to their daughter.

Jonathan continued to be impressed with the direct eye contact Paul maintained when they communicated. He knew they would do most of their bonding without words, as men do. They seemed to reach an understanding over the woman who lay motionless before them. He found it strange that his little Daisy lay unaware of the entire relationship building in her very presence. Jonathan had once read a quote which said, "In the midst of all of our planning life happens." He realized life moved forward today for Daisy, even while she slept away. This made him wonder what she might have had planned for the day.

Chapter Ten:

THE CLINIC

Barbara and Daisy insisted they could attend to their minor injuries, but those who came to their aid dropped them off at the clinic's front stoop. Standing at the glass double doors, a nurse greeted them and bid them to come right in. The doctor wanted to see them.

Daisy didn't like needles or pills and thought all medicine tasted funny. Now she sat alone in the waiting room of the local Wellness Station as the nurse had directed Barbara in first. While sitting in the waiting room, Daisy had been instructed to file the usual medical form attached to a clipboard before seeing the doctor. She used her yellow number-two pencil to begin filling out the form with the appropriate personal information. As she was just beginning to write her name, the nurse announced her as the next patient, "Delores Anne Zookes."

Daisy stood and entered the same doorway Barbara walked through. "That's funny," thought Daisy, "how did she know my name?"

Passing the nurse on her way, she read the nametag—Nurse Paula Hollands.

Nurse Hollands smiled saying, "Doctor A. Fairfield is ready to see you now."

She showed Daisy into a small room with a desk and two chairs. Rays of light beamed in through a huge side window overlooking a fishpond and a well-manicured garden. Daisy hadn't completed the form, but the nurse took hold of the clipboard procuring it for the doctor.

In a moment, a short man entered the small room wearing a white coat and a stethoscope. He wore a headband with an old fashioned magnifying piece attached. He gave her a warm, professional greeting and sat down in a chair opposite her.

The doctor proceeded to read from Daisy's uncompleted form on the clipboard provided to him from the nurse.

"Now let's see here, it states your full name as Delores Anne Zookes and that you reside at the Ammen's Apartment Building Unit 5, on Fifth Avenue, in Indianapolis, Indiana 53601. Is that correct so far?" asked the doctor. Daisy stared at him in disbelief, since she hadn't provided this information onto the form.

He continued, "Your date of birth is May 16th and that would make your present age 28 years old. Your height is five foot four inches tall. For your weight, you stated here that it is none of my business. Well, Ms. Zookes, if we are going to be that way about it." The doctor looked her over with suspicion. He read the form so fast; Daisy didn't have a chance to ask him where or how he had gotten any of the information.

"Let's proceed," the doctor went on. "The next question asked if you smoke? It says on the form, you only smoke when you have had a few too many." With that the doctor raised his eyebrows.

Daisy looked at the doctor with apprehension.

Clearing his throat, he read the next question, "Let's see now; do you drink alcohol and if yes, how much?" He read the answer, "Only at happy hour." With a serious tone he asked her, "Why aren't you happy?"

Daisy sprang from her chair as she blurted, "But I am happy. Where did you get those answers?"

"Now, now, all right. There, there Miss. Please don't get alarmed," said the doctor with a calming voice, while motioning for her to sit back down.

He proceeded to the next question. "Do you take or use any street drugs, now or ever? The answer states, you did experiment a little in your younger days. Oh?" questioned the doctor as he eyed her inquisitively.

Daisy reached across to where he had placed the form and clipboard, demanding to look at it. She noticed the form's questions were unanswered; therefore, how did he come by his answers? She stared at him, trying to understand how he knew the answers to the many questions pertaining to her private life. Perplexed, she looked down at her folded contained hands now resting on her lap.

"Well, you might as well go on," she said to the doctor.

He proceeded, "Are you using any over-the-counter drugs or prescribed medications at this time? Your answer, yes, birth control." The doctor asked, "Have you spoken to your mother about this?"

Daisy questioned his reasoning, "How old do you think I am?"

The doctor quipped right back, "Why? Did you lie on the form where it says that you are only twenty-eight?"

Daisy couldn't believe the uncanny manner he demonstrated in his responses to the supernaturally supplied albeit truthful answers of the questions.

This thought went through her mind, "I've supplied answers to these very same questions many times before at my usual doctor visits. But having someone supplying the correct answers in such a simple fashion is making me feel vulnerable. It's as if I am being examined under the eye of his large, goofy, magnifying headpiece."

However, Daisy's next inner thought surprised her, "Isn't this what a doctor is supposed to do, to take the necessary time to provide a full, open, and honest examination of the patient?" The thought intrigued her and she missed his next question.

The doctor repeated, "It asked you to rate your pain between one to ten. It states that you rate Ted Strain your number one pain!"

Daisy chortled saying, "You would feel the same way if you knew my boss."

"Oh," said the doctor. Then he took out the infamous wooden tongue suppressor and instructed Daisy to open up her mouth and say, "AAH."

"AAAAHHHH," obeyed Daisy.

"Mmmmm, I thought so," said the doctor. Then he told her, "Stick out your tongue."

Daisy did as she was told. The doctor asked, "Do you do that very often?"

She pulled her tongue back in and said "What? "

"Stick out your tongue at people," piped the doctor.

"Unbelievable," said Daisy as she sat back in her chair, folding her arms and crossing her legs.

After a moment of silence, she viewed the doctor and saw his big, warm smile. They both started to laugh at the humor of the whole escapade. She knew the doctor hadn't asked her anything out of the ordinary; it just seemed silly to have the doctor ask and supply all of the questions along with the answers.

Daisy unfolded her crossed limbs and started to relax in the doctor's presence.

"Well," said the doctor, "I'd say the diagnosis looks so so, but your sole prognosis will depend on how well you respond to the expedition into Niv and the prescription I am prescribing for you."

“Hey, wait a minute,” exclaimed Daisy sitting up straight, “A prescription for what? Why you haven’t even looked at my scraped knee or ask me about the accident. Say what kind of a doctor are you anyway?”

The doctor straightened in his chair replying, “I’m a licensed practicing physician. I check people over, examine their problematic lives, and prescribe what they need.”

He wrote out a script on a prescription pad and said, “Now Delores, you take this down the hall to the pharmacy and they will fill it for you. Thanks for stopping by, and I do hope you improve.”

Before Daisy could comment he rose from his chair and exited the room.

Daisy could see Nurse Hollands working behind the counter. She stood and exited the small room just as the nurse looked up and pointed down the hall stating, “The pharmacy is located at the end of the hall on the right. You can’t miss it.”

With that, Daisy walked down the hall with the all-knowing doctors script in hand.

When she came upon the pharmacy window, she saw Barbara leaning over the counter talking and laughing with the pharmacist.

“And how are you today?” he asked Daisy, upon pulling the script out of her hand.

An overhead sign flashed in the background: “Laughter

Does Good Like a Medicine Pharmacy." The man said, "The names Zeb, I'm the pharmacist. Barbara tells me that you and her were in a little mishap on a scooter."

Upon seeing Barbara, Daisy felt a little better. She sensed the pharmacist would at least take time to talk about their mishap, which brought them here in the first place. After the examination or whatever one would call it with Doctor Fairfield, she felt a tad bit exposed after the supplied answers to the vulnerable questions. Now she hoped to retrieve some answers; and with that she pulled out her pink notebook along with the yellow number-two pencil protruding from her back pocket.

Zeb continued, "Your script states you are in need of a good dose of medicine. Well you've come to the right place."

"You are going to enjoy this part of the clinic's visit," said Barbara.

Daisy shrugged her shoulders and awaited the pharmacist's directions.

Zeb proceeded to tell her and Barbara a joke that started out with the words, "Did you hear the one about?" When he got to the punch line, he and Barbara were laughing as two school chums.

Barbara noticed Daisy's uneasiness and put an arm around her shoulder saying, "Zeb's a good friend, and he enjoys making people laugh. We'll just indulge him for a while and then be on our way, Okay?"

Then she introduced her, "By the way Zeb, this is Delores.

Her friends call her Daisy. She and Spotty are hiking over into the city."

Zeb replied, "Welcome to Niv, Daisy. I hope you have a nice visit while you are here."

Daisy softened as he welcomed her. She suspected he wanted her to feel at home; therefore, she decided to drop her skepticism. She shook Zeb's outstretched hand and stated her willingness to receive his obvious banter of jokes, which he proceeded to do. In everyday settings, Daisy found it difficult to drop her guard around strangers. Now as the Provincial Wellness Clinic operated its medicinal work, she slowly began to open the door of her heart welcoming these strangers into her life.

Zeb told Daisy he would have her prescription filled in no time flat.

"Alright," said Daisy.

Zeb scratched his head and said; "The doctor wrote you a prescription for ten dosages."

"Ten dosages of what?" asked Daisy.

Barbara giggled and said, "Oh, you'll see."

Zeb scratched his head again as he spoke, "Let's see now. Daisy, for your first dosage, I know: What happens when you throw a clock in the air?" He looked at the girls and answered, "Time's up."

Barbara chuckled, while Daisy looked puzzled. She wondered if this pharmaceutical visit would be even sillier than

Doctor Fairfield's examination.

Zeb spoke again, "Dosage number two: Why did the cabinet go to the psychiatrist?" Zeb waited and when the two girls shook their shoulders not knowing the answer he said, "Because, it kept talking to its shelf."

This brought a smile to both of their faces. Daisy thought how funny and crazy to be telling jokes for a dose of medicine.

The next joke Zeb told was dosage number three, "What has lots of eyes but can't see?"

"A potato," he yelled, and went right on to the next one.

"Dosage number four: Why did the watch go on vacation?" he paused.

"Because it needed to unwind," and he grinned away at the two girls.

He continued, "Alright Daisy, now for dosage number five, this one is a little longer than the others. Here goes: A woman went to her psychiatrist and said, "Doctor, I want to talk to you about my husband. He thinks he's a refrigerator." "That's not bad," said the doctor. "It's a rather harmless problem." "Well, maybe," replied the lady, "But he sleeps with his mouth open and the light keeps me awake."

By the time Zeb finished dosage number five, all three were laughing. Zeb continued. "Okay ladies, dosage number six: What has a tail and a head but no body?" He answered, "A coin."

"Dosage number seven: What did the elevator say to the

other elevator? I think I'm coming down with something." Again they chuckled and laughed.

Zeb called out jokes as though he were reading them from a book. He said, "Dosage number eight: Patient: Doctor, Doctor, I feel like a pair of curtains. Doctor: Then pull yourself together."

When they came to dosage number nine they were in stitches. Zeb proceeded, "Dosage number nine: Nurse: Doctor, there is an invisible man in the waiting room.

Doctor: Tell him I can't see him."

In unison the three laughed all the more.

Then Zeb came to Daisy's last dose of medicine saying, "And for your last dose of medicine, number ten: Patient: Doctor I need help. I can never remember what I just said.

Doctor: When did you first notice the problem? Patient: Notice what problem."

Zeb smiled from ear to ear as the two girls wiped away the tears. They both collapsed into chairs positioned along the pharmacy hallway. Daisy grasped her aching side from laughing so long and hard.

Zeb stood in the pharmacy window looking pleased with the results of the medicinal dosages. Once the girls pulled themselves together, Zeb stated in his pharmaceutical voice, "Daisy, as usual, with all medications some common side effects could result, such as, giddiness, lightheadedness, a merry heart, or even new life. Should one feel overwhelmed with relief and develop a contagious smile, then the patient should share and report any or all of these side effects with friends and family members as soon as possible, as they may not be experiencing any of these within their daily lives."

This brought another round of laughter as Daisy and Barbara rose from the chairs. Daisy remembered her scraped knee. She pulled up her pants leg to see if it would need anything. The injury to her knee had long since vanished. Shrugging her shoulders, Daisy looked toward Barbara and said, "Oh well." She also noticed the uncomfortable feelings she experienced between her and the doctor had dissipated. She made a mental note to take an inventory of her life and review these very same questions. She would write these thoughts within her notebook.

After saying goodbye to Zeb, the pharmacist, Barbara and Daisy headed back to the main front desk where they had first entered the clinic.

On their way to the front desk, Daisy read the headings over the clinic doorways along with the doctor's names: Proverbial Cosmetic Surgery, Renewing the Mind Mental Health Ward, Heart Specialists - Dr. K. Transformation, Internist – PHD B. Cleansed, Residing Residents on Staff – Cecil M. Faithing and Alfred D. Uberkammt.

"What an unusual medical clinic," thought Daisy, but she did feel better and the medicinal dosages had done their job.

While checking out at the front desk, Daisy watched a

young boy approach Nurse Hollands. Barbara whispered into her ear about the boy being the caretaker of the clinic's Puppy Ward.

This information piqued Daisy's interest and she said, "I love puppies. Could we visit the puppy ward?"

As Barbara spoke with Daisy, Nurse Hollands noticed the boy's inquisitiveness about the newcomer. The nurse said, "Toni, I would like you to meet Barbara's new friend Delores Anne Zookes."

"Hello," said Daisy walking over to the young adolescent boy. He greeted her in return. Then she added, "My friends call me Daisy. You can call me that too."

The boy smiled and with a playful shove he pushed Barbara aside, as she had been pulling at his shirttails and arm.

The nurse reminded him, "Toni, it is getting late. Have you completed your puppy count for the day?" He gave an affirmative response.

Barbara said to Nurse Hollands, "I think it would be good for Daisy to tour the Puppy Ward. However, it's getting late and I must be getting back to my place. Daisy, I suggest you should consider staying at the clinic for the evening."

She noticed how it thrilled Toni to know that Daisy would be his guest, and could see Nurse Hollands pleasure at the idea too. Having settled the matter, Barbara said she would inform Spotty about Daisy's plan to spend the evening at the clinic.

“Spotty has been resting on a branch just outside the clinic’s door,” Nurse Hollands said.

“Thanks Nurse Hollands,” replied Barbara, “and don’t worry Daisy, Spotty will agree with you staying and visiting the Puppy Ward. I will share with him your plans to spend the evening.” She bade her goodbyes, and once outside she told Spotty of Daisy’s plans.

Since they had arrived at the clinic, Spotty stayed perched on a tree branch at the entrance of the clinic keeping watch. He had sense to post guard and to watch out for the Sly One. He blamed the scooter mishap on this wretched creature, for he knew he possessed evil intentions of keeping visitors side-tracked. Spotty had had similar experiences before with the Sly One’s attempts to thwart a visitor’s plan to reach the city of Niv.

Chapter Eleven:

ALOEWISHISH

The next day, Darla popped in during her lunch break to see how Daisy faired. She noticed how the medical staff took a liking to the Zookers, as they were a patient, undemanding couple. She suspected most families under these circumstances tended to be pushy and insistent with the medical staff. During her short visit, various staff members stopped in to check on Daisy's progress and to chit chat with the Zookers.

Darla enjoyed meeting Daisy's mother, Martha. The two hit it off and found they had much in common. They both enjoyed arts and crafts along with creating their own homemade interior designs. Since this had been Darla's forté, Strain had hired her to write articles for various home furnishings, interior-decorating, and arts and crafts magazines. The Martha Stewart-type magazines and TV programs had become a multi-million dollar business. Therefore, Darla accumulated plenty of work and projects to provide articles with the numerous magazines under contract with Strain.

"How did you and Daisy meet, Darla?" Martha asked.

"Daisy and I were both hired about the same time. Our cubicles were adjacent to one another on the eleventh floor. One thing led to another and we developed a solid friendship."

"It must be difficult to work for a man as demanding as Mr. Strain."

"All employees of the Hannah and Rhutkers JC Publishing Company tend to be inundated with work," Darla explained. "We are always busy researching material for various stories for the multi-magazine firms Mr. Strain supports. It's a good job and it does pay well. I have to admit; to be working on the eleventh floor in the Benson Building has been a dream come true for most everyone in its employ."

Martha changed the subject and asked, "Do you know where Daisy's apartment is located? I don't want to burden Tulip with this responsibility as well."

"Oh that's alright Martha. I have a spare key to her apartment. Plus, I had already spoken with Paul about taking care of Daisy's cat as well."

" I forgot all about her pet cat. Oh my, I do hope the cat will be all right," said Martha.

"No need to worry about the cat. I have a cat of my own, and it will be my pleasure to entertain her cat for a change."

"Thank you very much for helping us. Daisy is lucky to have made such a good friend. I have enjoyed talking with you and getting to know you."

Darla hugged Martha and softly iterated, "I'm glad too. I

just hope and pray Daisy will soon be back to her old self again." At that the two women pushed away their tears and sat quietly next to Daisy's bed until Darla had to return to work.

Later that evening, Darla used the extra set of keys to go into Daisy's apartment on Fifth Avenue. She entered the luxurious Ammen's apartment building and rode the elevator to the third floor. In the spacious hallway stood high-end furniture pieces, and modern art adorned the walls. The rent rose steeply with each floor because of the spectacular panorama of the city one could view from the balconies.

Daisy could afford to live here because she stuck to a strict budget, which enabled her to afford the upscale, small Fifth Avenue apartment, whereas Darla resided in a typical middle class apartment in the Candon Boulevard apartment complex across from Michelangelo's Ice Cream Parlor. She worked at the ice cream parlor part-time to help offset her crazy spending habits. The ice cream parlor served as a coffee shop, ice cream parlor, and yuppie bookshop. Young professionals enjoyed the atmosphere and used it as a place to discuss politics, work, and the latest fashions. Darla appreciated Daisy's friendship. They both got along well and enjoyed the comfort of their friends, the security of their jobs, and the excitement of living in a busy downtown metropolis.

Tonight, Darla's mission consisted of watering the plants and feeding Daisy's beloved cat, Aloewishish.

Being a true cat lover, Daisy had several pictures on

display of her beloved Aloewishish. Her white, longhaired, playful Persian cat had a gentle disposition. After feeding her and giving her some much-needed attention, Darla set about watering the plants.

Once finished with the tasks, Darla decided to sit down in the living room and rest her weary feet. In the marble foyer on her way into the building, she had retrieved the mail protruding from Daisy's mailbox. She had set it on the multi-tiled coffee table along with the keys. Darla leafed through the magazines from the stack of mail.

With her interest in cats, she chose a magazine entitled *Cats* to browse through. Highlighted on the cover of the magazine, she read an article outlining the many wild cats listed as endangered species.

Darla began reading about the large striped bengal tiger from India, Bangladesh, Nepa, Bhutan, and Burma. This cat remains in danger of extinction due to over-hunting by poachers.

Next the article listed another endangered cat, the cheetah, which is the fastest land animal. From South and Central America, the Jaguar has become an endangered species due to loss of habitat and being over-hunted by man. The widely-distributed wild cat known as the leopard has also been ranked among the threatened species due to loss of habitat, loss of prey, and over-hunting. And the fierce Lynx cat that lives deep in pine forests and thick scrub of North America and Eurasia has sadly been added to the list of endangered species.

"Unbelievable," said Darla, as she continued to read about the solitary, beautiful snow leopard of the snowy central mountains of Asia. This cat remains in danger of extinction due to loss of habitat, loss of prey, and over-hunting. Imagine, she thought, only a few snow leopards are left in the wild.

Continuing her read, she learned that as few as four hundred magnificent siberian tigers roam the wild. As the largest member of the cat family, these huge, territorial cats can be found in the Amur-Ussuri region of Siberia (in northeastern Russia) and in northern China and Korea.

Finally, the article ended listing as endangered the Puma, also known as the cougar, mountain lion, panther, or catamount. These fierce cats live deep in deciduous forests, rain forests, grasslands, and deserts of North America and South America. These solitary animals purr but cannot roar. They are, however, excellent jumpers, climbers and swimmers. Like all of the others, they are an endangered species due to loss of habitat and over-hunting by man.

After reading the article and because of her love for

cats, Darla felt led to do something about their endangerment. This article struck a chord deep within her soul, and she planned to dig further and research more about this subject. She figured once she had accumulated enough information and had developed a premise, she would meet with Strain to discuss a plan of action. If it meant more business for the company, he would encourage her to develop a story or to do something on that line. Wishing Daisy had been available, she would like to have spoken with her and shared the urgency washing over her concerning the wild cats' preservation.

Darla finished her chores at the apartment. Taking one last look around, she locked the front door. She decided to drive to Michelangelo's and visit with some friends. They would want an update on Daisy's condition, and she looked forward to a good cup of coffee.

As she drove away from Daisy's apartment building, the endangered cat article played on her mind. Maybe this type of writing venture would provide an opportunity to do more on her part in helping to improve the world. With that settled in her mind, she headed off to Michelangelo's ice cream parlor with the magazine tucked away in her oversized handbag.

Chapter Twelve:

HOPE

The Puppy Ward was located down a long corridor in the west end wing of the wellness station. Antonio Salderonada ran the ward and was the Puppy Ward Coordinator. Toni, maintained a regimented schedule making sure to deliver each puppy to the designated patient.

Born with an adorable, unassuming nature, puppies can evoke a special feeling within the patients. Their waggy-tail presence can bring out an instant love. Many of the patients who ventured through the province's wellness station needed what a puppy's disposition could provide. Therefore, the treatment required for the patient's condition determined a puppy's assignment.

Thus, part of Toni's duty consisted of escorting the prescribed puppy to the specific patient's room per a doctor's request. The treatments varied from patient to patient. For example, a patient diagnosed with loneliness would be prescribed a puppy accelerating and in need of companionship and attention. If a patient had been dealing with a broken heart, then a puppy excelling in lots of licking would be offered as good medicine. Whatever the need, most patients just seemed to want to cuddle and hold onto the puppy while expressing brokenness, pain, or suffering. Any and all who came to the wellness center left with a renewed spirit and maybe a few torn slippers if they utilized the puppy treatment.

In their innocence, the puppies possessed the uncanny ability to soften a man's hard outer shell. The puppies provided a good source for the patient yearning to be a caretaker or a caregiver. Since the puppies required plenty of care, those overwhelmed with the feeling of uselessness could visit the clinic and were permitted to assist Toni within the puppy ward. Each and every day, the puppies preformed many services at the clinic for various patients.

Toni explained all of this to Daisy while providing a general tour of the Puppy Ward.

"I have seventy-seven puppies under my care. Each one represents a different breed, and I had the privilege of naming each one."

"I am amazed at how fresh the ward smells in spite of so many puppies living here," said Daisy.

Toni laughed, "We have plenty of trees placed about as indoor house plants, because skynthesis is at work in this ward twenty-four seven."

Daisy squealed with delight each time she encountered a different puppy.

Toni recognized the joy springing forth from Daisy. "I often see this same reaction as a patient interacts with a puppy. Even the most stiff-necked person will bend down and play with a puppy. This therapy softens the hardened heart." He added, "The clinic has found with the softening of many hearts comes an overall increase of humility, kindness, and generosity throughout the region."

As Daisy was surrounded by the puppies he said, "The Puppy Ward is one of the busiest wings in the clinic; many to receive love, some to give of themselves, while others are learning to simply let go."

"What becomes of the puppies once they become mature dogs?" asked Daisy.

Though Toni had never been asked that question before, he explained, "These puppies never age. Their sole purpose and duty within the province is to provide a service of love and nurturing for the patients. It wouldn't make any sense for them to age, because then they would lose their joy and purpose. The King created them to be puppies."

Even among puppies this King is mentioned, thought Daisy.

"Don't you like the puppies, Daisy?" Toni asked.

"Oh, yes Toni, I do. They are the cutest things in the world. It's just that puppies don't stay puppies for very long where I come from."

Toni never gave it a second thought. He assured her that

even if a puppy did grow up and become a full grown dog; it would be loved and well taken care of in the province.

"Besides," he interjected, "What could be more faithful or loyal than one's own dog."

"True, so very true," replied Daisy looking over all the puppies at her feet waiting to be loved by her.

Toni spoke with each and every puppy with gentleness and patience. They all took their turns as he directed each one to it's own personal pillow with its name embroidered onto the fabric.

Daisy ambled over to clipboards hanging on the light gray, plastered walls. The plaster resembled a type of marble material. She couldn't make out the texture, as it looked like paint but then appeared to be a marble substance. Many different textures and features existed within the province. The puppy ward floor consisted of a deep grayish blue hue with dark blue specks that shone like glass. Daisy thought it could have been some type of acrylic finish. The floor wasn't slippery to walk on. Cushions had been strewn about the area to relax and sit on.

She went back to studying the list on the clipboard. It contained every dog's breed and name. Other lists attached to clipboards hung next to this main list. These lists charted the daily postings of the room assignments. The postings changed daily. Toni used a rotating scheduled as all of the puppies were used throughout a given week at one time or another.

Toni demonstrated how he kept track of the postings, and described in detail how he had designed the charts for feeding, grooming, and walking periods.

Daisy observed the pride he took in running the Puppy Ward at the Wellness Station.

Evening had set in and Toni had to complete the final puppy count for the day.

Daisy sat on a huge brown cushion petting a Cape Hunting puppy named Tenderhearted. A beagle puppy named Hope stayed close at Toni's feet while he finished his duties. The tri-colored beagle puppy had a definitive white fur line running between her eyes; it stemmed straight from her nose to her forehead. Once he finished his work, Toni checked to make sure that each dog lay on his or her cushion for the evening. On instinct, most of the puppies scurried over to their pillows without being directed. Daisy found the sight endearing.

He and Daisy ate a light snack the clinic had provided on Toni's desk area. They munched away as Toni elaborated more about the work and services at the clinic and the Puppy Ward. He told Daisy, "Under no circumstances should a door be left opened where the puppies are concerned. They have a tendency to go exploring, so the door to the puppy ward and the outer door to the clinic must remain closed at all times. This is why I do the all-important final puppy count every evening."

"I'll be sure to close both doors if I should venture out of the ward during my visit," Daisy assured him.

She liked the boy and thought him to be quite responsible for someone his age.

This prompted her to ask, "Your mother and father must have instructed you well with tasks and chores around the house, because you keep things so well organized. How long have you been in Niv?"

He answered, "I never knew my parents. The day of my birth, a neighbor found me left on the doorstep of a local doctor's home. I have been in Niv ever since. The King of Niv took care of me. Later, he placed me in charge of the puppies. Working and living in the province is the only life I have ever known. The clinic staff remain my closest family."

Toni spoke way into the evening and fell asleep with the little beagle Hope resting in his arms. Once Daisy noticed him sleeping, she decided to take a walk outside. Reflecting on the day, she planned to enter personal information into her notebook. Plus, she looked forward to some alone time while contemplating all the things that had transpired on her journey through Niv today.

Being ever so quiet, Daisy crept out of the expansive ward without waking Toni or any of the snoozing puppies. Once she got to the door, she turned the handle and made a quick exit into the hallway. She had her notebook and yellow number-two pencil in hand as she went along. Admiring all the sleeping puppies as she tiptoed, she failed to notice the little figure following at her footsteps. Upon shutting the inner door, she thought it best to continue tiptoeing while heading toward the outer door. Certain the puppies were secure, she propped the outer door open with a small stone to prevent it from locking. She thought a puppy couldn't get through such a small opening. Unbeknownst to her, the doors in Niv didn't lock.

Hope the beagle had followed close at Daisy's heel. She waited by the inner door, watching Daisy place a stone to keep the outer door ajar. Outside, Daisy found a solitary grassy area to contemplate and journal the events of the day within the notebook. She became engrossed in remembering all that transpired with the scooter, Barbara, and the clinic. Thus, she failed to catch Hope the beagle squirm her little body through the small opening of the outside door. Daisy made entry after entry into the notebook for over an hour. Being a professional writer, she had learned early in her career that making an excessive amount of notes proved essential for producing a good read.

Satisfied with the entries, she placed the yellow number-two pencil back into her back pocket. She took a walk to the front of the clinic and found Spotty sound asleep. Thinking it best not to disturb him, she walked back to the door she had left ajar. Once inside, she double-checked, making sure the outer door closed behind her.

Close to where she had sat writing rested the sleeping beagle. In a nearby meadow, the Sly One had been watching and waiting for such an opportunity. He hurried to find some puppy treats to tempt Hope the puppy away from the security of the clinic. This imposter of kindness had been trailing Daisy and Spotty since the gate where Daisy had encountered the butterflies. He didn't hesitate to jump at another chancc to thwart Daisy's journey. He had seen the little unattended puppy wander out the door behind Daisy. After waking the puppy, the Sly One set scrumptious tiny morsels of food on a path leading her in the direction of the woods. Hope wagged her tail and scurried along the path looking forward to the treats. She had to move her puppy legs fast to keep up with the one dropping the morsels. His hideousness camouflaged and seeing only the Sly One's back, Hope followed the trail of goodies deep into the woods.

Toni rose early and began his daily care of the puppies. Performing a quick puppy tally, he became alarmed to find one missing. His beloved Hope had failed to show up for the count, causing his heart to sink. Startled and worried he made an immediate search of the general area.

Waking up, Daisy noticed the commotion amongst the puppies and could tell Toni appeared agitated.

With remorse he told her, "Hope is missing. I searched the inside of the Wellness Station and couldn't find her. Did you by any chance leave the clinic during the night?"

"After you fell asleep," she explained," I went outside to write in my notebook. I took the necessary precautions of watching for a stray puppy, plus I closed the inner door. However, I did leave the outer door ajar for fear of becoming locked out of the clinic."

"Oh Daisy, I should have told you. The clinic doors don't lock. Hope must have snuck out while you were busy writing."

Daisy felt horrible. A knot formed in the pit of her stomach as she realized what she had done. She drifted back to a time in her youth when she babysat for a neighbor. She had forgotten to turn off a stovetop burner after warming the infant's bottle. When the child's parents returned home later in the evening, they brought this to her attention. Imagining the unthinkable, she pictured the house catching on fire. Seeing the distress on Toni's face brought these same dreadful feelings to the surface. She wanted so much to make things right.

"We will have to go look for Hope and not stop until we find her. Without food, I doubt she would have gone very far. Unless, oh no, someone could be leading her astray, " he said. With heightened concern, Toni knew about the Sly One and realized he would stoop to any trick to thwart the peace with the visitors in Niv.

After checking the premises of the clinic, Toni and Daisy decided to walk down the path and into the woods. He had asked Nurse Hollands to watch over the other 76 puppies, while he and Daisy ventured into the countryside in search of Hope.

Daisy didn't take the time to tell Spotty of their plans. She left a note and gave it to Nurse Hollands, letting Spotty know they would return upon finding Hope. Toni had seen Spotty asleep in the tree as he searched the immediate grounds of the clinic, but chose not to arouse him. He had a mission to find Hope and nothing else mattered at the moment.

With a heavy heart, Daisy followed Toni into the woods. Toni set about with a determination that overshadowed her fears. She could see a serious nature arise in this young man who already outshone others of his age.

How distressing, thought Daisy, I am responsible for losing Hope. They searched and searched up and down the paths and deep into the woods.

After an hour or so of searching, Daisy and Toni became discouraged. They stopped for a moment taking time to scan an area, most often unsure of which direction to follow. Coming to a junction where two paths intersected, forming a cross pattern, reminded Toni of a previous encounter he had with the King of Niv.

"Daisy," said Toni, "I remember the King promising he could meet any need, at any place, and anytime. He shared this promise with me. He said to ask and you shall receive. I think we need to stop searching and take some time to ask him for help."

It didn't surprise Daisy to hear Toni speaking about the King. So many of her conversations within the province had led to this King of Niv. She couldn't be sure if this king could help or not, but what could it hurt to comply with Toni's wishes? Since guilt of losing Hope clouded her judgment, she had failed to come up with a solution. Daisy replied with all the inspiration she could muster, "Any solution would be better than no solution at all. Let's go for it, Toni. How do we go about calling on this King for help?"

"Let's just ask him right where we are to send some help. If the King is listening like he said, then he'll provide. I think a unified effort would be our best chance," said Toni.

Anything sounded good to Daisy. At the moment she felt weak and insecure. This part of her adventure into Niv she would have preferred to forgo. In predicaments similar to this, she would wish to wake up and find it had only been a bad dream. The fault rested with her and she didn't want Hope to remain lost or to be hurt. "Toni you start," she urged, "and I'll join and be in agreement with whatever you ask."

Toni began talking in a prayerful way, "Dear King, sir, we are in great need of your help. Precious Hope the puppy, my little beagle is lost." (At this Toni got quiet trying to hide his tears, then he continued.) "Could you please send some help right away? I'm sorry for the mishap. I know you put me in charge of the puppies, but one got away. I need your help in finding her. Daisy and I would appreciate it if you would somehow help us to locate her." Then he added, "And by the way, thanks for visiting last month with me and the puppies at the clinic. We were glad to see you and grateful that you brought some treats too."

Even though Toni did not want to cry in front of Daisy, she heard him sniffle.

Daisy remained silent all the while agreeing with Toni's request to the King of Niv for help. She did keep muttering under her breath, "Oh please help, whoever you are, please find the puppy." Her voice became choked as a frog caught in her throat, as she too had to fend off the tears.

She knew she didn't measure up to this remarkable young man. Her biggest concerns had been designer clothes, stories for work, and her climb up the corporate publishing ladder. Toni on the other hand reminded her of Paul Thornchen. Pulling at the gold chain around her neck, she remembered how morally responsible he remained, aside from being patient, kind, and loving. Paul kept his life simple - always appreciative of the small things, the everyday things.

Now this young boy Toni, even in a time of trouble, offered a note of thanks to the King. She chided herself and realized she needed to mend her selfish ways.

She bore the fault concerning Hope, and she had overheard Toni apologizing in her stead to the King while he asked for help. This young kid willingly took the blame for her mistake. Her expedition into the province of Niv had now become much more than a lesson about endangered species and a note-taking procedure for an adventure story.

A huge wind whipped her hair onto her face and broke her thought process. Pushing her hair back, another wind blew even fiercer than the first.

Toni jumped on top of a log and called to her, "Do you hear that?"

Daisy listened.

Then the strong wind blew again and the sound Toni had first heard became clearer and more distinct. "Why, it's the howling of a beagle," exclaimed Toni — for he'd recognize her howl anywhere.

"Yippee," he cried, and off they went running into the direction of the howl. They came upon Hope and found her penned in by a barrier of stones that someone had placed in a circle. The two worked together. They broke down the barrier and set Hope free. Overcome with joy, the puppy jumped up and began licking Toni in the face, all the while wiggling her tail and body. Toni nuzzled her with his chin, thankful to have his little lost Hope back in his protective arms. He carried her out of the woods and back onto the path.

Hope howled and barked, excited to be with Toni. Relieved, Daisy put her arms around Toni and asked, "Please forgive me for failing to keep the door shut as you had requested."

"I forgive you, Daisy," Toni said straightaway.

Then he looked up toward the sky and said, "Thank you dear King for helping us find Hope".

Hope let out a beagle howl that sent the two of them laughing. They walked fast as they made their way back to the clinic. Spotty flew overhead spying the two walkers on one of the paths leading in the direction of the clinic.

He swooped down and said to them, "So there you are, I've been looking for you two."

"Oh Spotty," said Daisy, "are we glad! We, well I had left the door open at the clinic, which resulted in Hope getting lost, and now we have her back safe and sound. See."

Spotty quipped with a whistle, "Well I am glad to see that you have Hope back. Nurse Hollands told me about the lost puppy. Everyone at the clinic keeps asking for any updates. By the way, hello there Toni. I don't think we got to say hello yesterday."

"Hello Spotty," replied Toni. "Sorry I didn't wake you this morning. But we just had to go and look for Hope. I never meant for Daisy to leave the clinic without notifying you first."

While he spoke to Spotty he handed Hope, who had been squirming in his arms, over to Daisy. Daisy took her from Toni. She wanted to cuddle with the puppy and share her relief at having her back in their company. The puppy began to lick Daisy's face, as puppies do when they are happy and want to shower someone with love. Hearing an all-too-familiar voice, Daisy's eyes opened wide and she froze.

At the Trauma Center, Jonathan J. Zookers sat alone in the room next to his daughter's comatose body. With tenderness, he began wiping her face with a damp washcloth. His wife and Tulip had gone to the cafeteria for lunch, and he stole this first moment to be alone with his daughter since arriving in Indianapolis. Concerned as a father, he poured out the innermost feelings he had for his youngest family member. He said, "Oh my sweet, little precious Daisy Annie, your momma and I love you so much. We just want you to be sitting here with us, talking away, and telling us how things are, in your exasperating informative way." He wiped away a tear streaming down his elderly worn face and continued, "You know honey if I could, I'd send a hound to track you down so that I could bring you back from the world where you are; I guess somewhere between here and there." He stopped to blow his nose and continued, "The doctor says most people can hear when they are in a coma. I want you to know we are here for you. I love you Daisy Annie; you're my precious little flower." He continued to wash and caress her face with the damp washcloth, while uttering short, silent prayers.

Daisy snapped back to find the puppy still consumed with licking her face. She interrupted Spotty and Toni's conversation asking, " Did you both hear what I just heard?" They looked at her, shrugged their shoulders, and said they hadn't heard anything.

"Oh," responded Daisy, surprised at their unawareness of what just happened to her. She had recognized her father's voice. It gave her great comfort to know that somewhere from beyond, her Daddy had been looking out for her, especially at a time when she had lost Hope—or did she mean hope in the literal sense. She gave the puppy back to Toni and they continued on their way.

"Daisy," piped Spotty, "I think we should be getting back on course and make our way into the city."

"I sure did enjoy your visit, Daisy," said Toni, "and I am grateful we found Hope. Thanks for helping me to locate her. I know my way back to the wellness station from here. Why don't you both cut to the right at the next crossing? That will lead you back to the thoroughfare. Hope and I will be fine."

They said goodbye at the next juncture. Toni pressing Hope against his chest headed in the direction of the Wellness Station, Spotty and Daisy headed toward the thoroughfare and to the city of Niv.

The Puppy Ward Chart

	Breed	Name
1	Afghan Hound	Abundance
2	African Wild Dog	Alpha
3	Alaskan Malamute	Angel
4	American Eskimo Dog	Brilliance
5	American Foxhound	Champion
6	Anatolian Shepherd Dog	Compassion
7	Australian Cattle Dog	Cozy Pete
8	Basset Hound	Cuddles
9	Beagle	Hope
10	Bedlington Terrier	Encouragement
11	Belgian Malinois	Eternal
12	Bernese Mountain Dog	Ezra
13	Bichon Frise	Faith
14	Black Russian Terrier	Fearless
15	Bloodhound	Freedom
16	Border Collie	Friender
17	Borzoi	Fruitful Frank
18	Boston Terrier	Gaity
19	Boxer	Generous
20	Brittany	Gilead
21	Brussels Griffon	Giver
22	Bulldog	Glory
23	Canaan Dog	Goodness
24	Chesapeake Bay Retriever	Goshem
25	Chihuahua	Grace
26	Cape Hunting Dog	Tender-hearted

	Breed	Name
27	Chinese Shar-Pei	Haggai
28	Chow Chow	Hannah
29	Cocker Spaniel	Jake
30	Collie	Hessad
31	Dachshund	Danial
32	Dalmatian	Jesse
33	Doberman Pinscher	Jonah
34	English Springer Spaniel	Joyful
35	Finnish Spitz	Judah
36	French Bulldog	Buddy
37	German Shepherd Dog	King
38	Golden Retriever	Lillie Light
39	Great Dane	Lion
40	Great Pyrenees	Lovely
41	Greyhound	Luminous
42	Harrier	Lydia
43	Ibizan Hound	Maggie
44	Irish Setter	Malachi
45	Irish Wolfhound	Meekness
46	Italian Greyhound	Mercy
47	Japanese Chin	Micah
48	Komondor	Mickey Manna
49	Labrador Retriever	Moses
50	Lhasa Apso	Tiger
51	Maltese	Olive
52	Mastiff	Omega

	Breed	Name
53	Newfoundland	River
54	Norwegian Elkhound	Patience
55	Otterhound	Perfect
56	Papillon	Pete
57	Pekingese	Prince
58	Pointer	Queenie
59	Polish Lowland Sheepdog	Ransom
60	Pomeranian	Righteous
61	Poodle	Penny
62	Portuguese Water Dog	Ruth
63	Pug	Sacred Sammy
64	Rottweiler	Sarah
65	Saint Bernard	Nahum
66	Scottish Deerhound	Sinai
67	Shetland Sheepdog	Softie
68	Shih Tzu	Tigger
69	Siberian Husky	Splendor
70	Spinone Italiano	Star
71	Standard Schnauzer	Sunshine
72	Sussex Spaniel	Tamar
73	Swedish Vallhund	Truth
74	Tibetan Terrier	Wonders
75	Weimaraner	Zach
76	Whippet	Zeke
77	Yorkshire Terrier	Zerah

Chapter Thirteen:

RETURN TO THOROUGHFARE

Along the way, Daisy questioned Spotty asking, "Who would have led Hope the puppy far into the woods, fencing her in and leaving her abandoned."

Spotty said, "It had to have been the Sly One."

Daisy grimaced, "The Sly One; who is that?"

Spotty explained, "The Sly One if full of devilish tactics. His purpose in the province is to thwart and sidetrack the plans of any visitor. Therefore Daisy, you are no exception."

"Me," exclaimed Daisy, "Why would he be concerned with me."

"Within the province," Spotty explained, "we have an occasional encounter with the Sly One. His powerless attempts are limited in Niv; we find him more of a distraction than anything else."

"Should I be worried about him?"

"One need not worry, but I would pay a little more attention," said Spotty.

Daisy and Spotty continued walking along on Begin Again Thoroughfare, having a discussion about the variety of puppies at the wellness center.

Spotty proceeded to tell her about the African Wild Dog that is also known as the Cape Hunting Dog.

"This dog," he said, "has short, spotted fur with large ears, sharp eyes, and a keen sense of smell. With a life span of about eleven years, it can weigh between 45 and 80 pounds. This breed hunts in packs in Africa and can run over 30 miles an hour. Lions and leopards sometimes kill these dogs, but people have exterminated many of them. They have thought of them as pests and have brought them to the brink of extinction."

"This is horrible news."

Spotty began telling Daisy about many more African species endangered or threatened with extinction.

He said, " The African Elephant is the largest living land animal and has been added to the endangered list due to loss of habitat and poaching."

"Elephants are magnificent creatures, how sad."

"Yes," said Spotty continuing, "Did you know the oryx are long-horned antelopes from dry areas in Africa, Asia, and the Arabian Peninsula? They too are in danger of extinction because of over-hunting and disease. People tend to link them to the unicorn."

"I've often wondered about unicorns and what became of them," shared Daisy.

Spotty went on to say, "The swift running gazelles live in African herds. Did you know they could bounce on all four legs held in a stiff position? It's called pronking. They are located across North Africa, Southwest Asia and many of their fourteen species are also in danger of extinction."

"I never knew so many animals were endangered."

"Oh, many more have become endangered; every year more species get added to the list," he said. "Look at the gorilla, the great apes from Africa. They too are in danger of extinction."

Before Daisy could respond he spoke, "Even the jackass penguin also known as the African penguin has been affected. This small penguin is located off the coast of Southern Africa. The penguin's populations has been declining rapidly due to a reduction of its food supply (by over fishing), pollution (from oil tankers), egg harvesting by people, disease, and guano (bird droppings) removal from their nesting grounds for use as a fertilizer. Daisy, this is an ongoing concern."

"I never even heard of this type of Penguin."

"Did you ever hear of a near-threatened nocturnal, giraffe-like mammal from the African rainforests called the okapi, Daisy?" "This okapi (or "forest giraffe") is a solitary, giraffe-like mammal found in rainforests of the upper Congo River Basin in central Africa. Scientists only discovered this nocturnal animal in the early 1900s.

Spotty next told her about orangutans saying, "Also on the endangered species list is the Orangutan. The large intelligent, solitary, tree-dwelling ape lives in Southeast Asia on the islands of Borneo and Sumatra. All they want to do is swing from tree to tree. It's a shame to find them disappearing."

Daisy became saddened by all Spotty shared with her.

He finished his endangered dissertation saying, "The last one I will mention is the solitary nocturnal Aye-aye. This strange primate and mammal lives in the Madagascar rain forest, which is situated off the southeast coast of Africa.

After Spotty had bent Daisy's ear they traveled along in silence, as the information had a sobering effect on her. They walked quite a ways following the road making their way onward to the city. At a certain juncture in the road, Daisy remarked that she needed to rest. Her temples had begun pounding. She even felt lightheaded. Spotty did a quick check and they ventured off the road down a short path, coming to rest by a stream.

Chapter Fourteen:

BUTTERNUT PARADISE

At the stream's edge, Daisy and Spotty encountered a man dressed in an army uniform asleep under a butternut tree with his bicycle parked nearby. Daisy observed his uniform resembled a war era long before her time and appeared to be of a European nationality. His tall, black, shiny boots and his silver buttons had a military insignia inscribed on them. His military hat lay next to him and his mustache twitched under his nose every now and then. He had built a small stone fire and had been roasting a small pan full of nuts. The roasted nuts created a delightful aroma, which made her stomach growl. The green grass-covered banks added to the peaceful scene alongside the stream. The leaved trees had produced an abundance of nuts. Numerous low-lying shrubs and other plant life filled the region with protruding flowers scattered about. Daisy thought of her parents and how much they would have enjoyed this ideal botanical setting.

Daisy and Spotty had decided to slip away so as not to

disturb the man in uniform, when he awoke. He smiled a broad, toothy smile and sat up stretching his arms while he yawned.

"Good day," he said to the two visitors, "Would you like to join me and share in my butternut snack?"

"I'm sorry. We did not mean to awaken you," said Daisy.

"No problem, my lady," said the gentleman. "Glad to have the company. What are you and your feathered friend's names?"

Daisy and Spotty introduced themselves and told him that they were making their way into the city.

"My name is Staff Sergeant Jon Ashley Bloomenfield. I had been assigned to an Italian regiment in Spain. However, today, I work with Niv's provincial army. The others and I spend our days learning about the province's military tactics and methods. It's been an expeditious time for my detachment within the province. The King's military academy is extraordinary. I would have to say its training is exemplary, a well-designed military with sufficient training and well-equipped. His armies are more than capable to defeat any adversary. As a citizen who has elected to serve in his great military force, I have had the pleasure to encounter the utmost loyalty, honor, and respect ever displayed among troops." He stopped for a minute realizing he had been rambling on and said, "I do say, I brag about them all the time. Well, here I am going on and on about the province's military might and myself. I can tell your face appears a bit perplexed."

"You did go on a bit," said Daisy, "but I found it interesting. I am surprised to encounter a military person. As a visitor, I have been learning something new about this province all the time." She hesitated to ask, "But I have found the province to be quite peaceful, so it puzzles me see you in uniform. Do you in fact fight battles here in Niv?"

"Oh, my no. I don't even carry a weapon," said the staff sergeant emphatically. "My fellow comrades and I are immersed in learning and observing what the King had already set in place. I wear my uniform as a sign of pride for my country and the men of my regiment, because it is who I am. Ever since I was knee high to a grasshopper, I wanted to be a soldier. When I became of age, I enlisted into the Italian army. I served my country well. One day during a field maneuver, I came to be here in Niv." He smiled as he said these words and looked straight at Daisy. "So, tell me Miss Daisy, are you hungry?"

At that, Daisy turned her attention to the nuts roasting in the pan.

Then, Staff Sergeant Bloomenfield produced a flask containing fresh milk. He asked her is she preferred her milk warm or cold. He said, "I could warm it over the fire if you like."

By this time, Spotty had found a nice tree branch to nest on while the two exchanged pleasantries.

Daisy said, "Cold milk will be fine." Then she asked, "Is

milk the normal beverage of choice for grown men to drink in the province?"

The staff sergeant stated, "The milk in the province has been the best I have ever tasted. The cows and the goats roam free in the fields eating the choicest of grasses. Without question, their milk is the most delicious and nutritious drink."

He poured Daisy a cup full and she drank. She had to agree saying, "It's very full and rich. It has a malted milkshake consistency."

With his empty cup in hand, he invited Daisy to follow him as he approached a nearby tree. Huge honeybees flew in and around a nice-size hole in the tree's trunk. The honeybees moved away from the opening, granting the sergeant liberty to stick his cup inside the tree's hole. He filled it with a small amount of honey and nodded to Daisy as they walked back toward the small stone fire.

The staff sergeant explained to Daisy the history of the honeybee and the uncertainty of its survival. He said, "Scientists have noticed the unusual disappearance of honeybee colonies throughout North America. This has brought about a concern and has placed them on the endangered species list. Dependent upon bee's pollination, a dilemma has developed about North America's food supply. Did you know that Miss Daisy?"

Daisy shook her head answering, "No."

Back at the stone fire he spooned the honey over the roasting nuts. "The nuts will taste good with the refreshing milk," said the staff sergeant.

Daisy, studying the unusual stone fire asked, "How does the fire burn without adding wood?"

The staff sergeant showed her how the stones could be hit and scraped together, producing heat and fire. He demonstrated how to position the stones in a certain sequence, enabling them to remain burning red hot. He said, "Anyone could build a small campfire."

Daisy found the stone fire amazing and economical.

"Have you ever had butternuts before, since they were not as easy to come by these days?"

"I am familiar with butternuts as they grow in my home state of Pennsylvania," answered Daisy. "I did not know they were in short supply."

They supped together on the nuts and honey that he served on his metal field gear kept in his army knapsack. With the food consumed, they reclined against the butternut trees and sipped the milk he served from his army flask into the metal cups. As they reclined against the trees, Daisy noticed skynthesis taking effect. The leaves of the trees fluttered as though a breeze caused them to dance, but at the moment no breeze existed.

The scrumptious warm nuts and honey tasted even better with each and every bite. North American song birds started to sing and fly about in the nearby trees and bushes. A couple drank at the water's edge, as they too seemed to enjoy the stream and their surroundings.

Daisy found the staff sergeant's conversation interesting as he shared one story after another about his military exploits and travels. He was a good host. He spoke about the beauty of the stream. The staff sergeant even shared words his mother used to quote to him as a young lad. He confessed how they had given him peace of mind during Italy's war days. He said, "My friends, keep your minds on whatever is true, pure, right, holy, friendly, and proper. Don't ever stop thinking on what is truly worthwhile and worthy of praise."

Mesmerized by the scene, Daisy thought the words he spoke apropos for the setting, which lay all about them. She noted Spotty resting in the tree branch as she drifted off to sleep. Before she dozed, she made a mental note to jot this place down in her notebook calling it "Butternut Paradise."

Chapter Fifteen:

BIKING THE THOROUGHFARE

The three awoke to a commotion of voices as a group of bicyclists made their way on the path. Sergeant Rockingham and part of the squadron had come looking for him. The sergeant said to the staff sergeant, "We're expected back at the briefing center for a meeting. We knew we would find you camped out in the forest."

The group of jovial young men carried on in a playful manner. Their carefree behavior reminded Daisy of other young off-duty military personal she had encountered in downtown Indianapolis. This group joked about the staff sergeant traipsing off to explore the countryside. Bloomenfield's comrades knew he enjoyed the outdoors and would use any opportunity to sneak away on his bike and ride to this particular spot next to the stream.

The staff sergeant introduced his comrades, "Miss Daisy, I would like you to meet my friends and comrades: Sergeant

Rockingham, Private Nichols, Airman Ortley, Ensign Crosby, and Petty Officer Duran."

The men greeted Daisy as they tipped their military hats and berets.

"Oops, I almost forgot," said the staff sergeant as he pointed up towards the branches, "You all know Spotty."

With the formalities out of the way, the staff sergeant set about packing his gear and loading his bicycle.

Spotty chatted with the comrades and then asked, "Could you permit Daisy to ride along with Sergeant Rockingham on his bicycle built for two? After all, we're going in the same direction and this would aid in speeding up our journey to the city."

The staff sergeant said, "That's a splendid idea. I wish I had thought of it.

The briefing center lays further down the road past the main gate; therefore, we won't be entering the city. But, you are more than welcome to join us." Then he asked, "Can you pedal a bicycle, Miss?"

"Yes, I am a good cyclist, plus I feel well rested after our nap by the stream."

"Okay," said the sergeant. "Hop aboard."

The men had a second bicycle built for two and two of the comrades paired up. The bicyclists peddled the path back to the main thoroughfare. Daisy rode in the second seat behind Sergeant Rockingham on his bicycle built for two.

Determined to keep watch, Spotty kept the crew in sight while flying overhead.

As the group biked the Thoroughfare, they sang some of their troop's marching songs. Daisy found it easy to pedal the two-seater bike; she enjoyed their singing. Losing herself in the moment, she daydreamed as they sang. They broke free of the wooded area and rode past large open fields with sheep, cows, horses, and goats grazing in the pastures.

Caught up in the scenery and song, she began to hear background singing apart from these military comrades. A man's voice permeated her mind, warmed her heart, and invaded her daydream.

At that very moment back at the Indiana Trauma Center, Paul stroked her forehead and sang a soft simple tune close to her face. He sang, "Daisy, Daisy give me your answer do, I'm half crazy all for the love of you. It won't be a stylish marriage, I can't afford a carriage, but you'll look sweet, upon the seat, of a bicycle built for two."

Paul's love and concern for her mounted as another day passed. Today, in particular, he found himself near tears as she lay so still in the hospital bed.

A nurse entered the room to check Daisy's monitors,

breaking the spell of the moment between Paul and Daisy.

The sergeant noticed how quiet she had become and asked, "Are you alright back there with pedaling?"

His questioning brought her back to the open fields and to the singing group up ahead as they pedaled their way on the road.

"Fine," she said, then asked, "Why do they let the animals run loose in the countryside? Shouldn't someone put a fence around the fields to protect the animals? What's to prevent them from running away?"

The sergeant asked, "Where do you think the animals would run away to? They have plenty of good grazing space in the province's green pastures."

Daisy said, "Yes, I guess so, but animals are known to roam. Back home all animals are to be kept on a leash or fenced. This keeps them from wandering away and it protects them from harm."

"Oh, and what harm might that be?" asked the sergeant.

She said, "Hey, you are in the army. Aren't you protecting the people in this province from imminent danger? Therefore, wouldn't it be only natural to want to also protect the animals from any injury or harm?"

The sergeant said, "The enlisted personal in the provincial army have a duty to serve the King. The province of Niv is a danger free zone; therefore, every citizen throughout the province remains shielded from all harm or danger. The King

has full knowledge of who and what comes through the gate at the entrance of the province." He asked, "Did you encounter the large open gate when you first started on your journey on Begin Again Thoroughfare?"

"Yes, I did. But..." responded Daisy.

The sergeant interrupted, "Because of the King's gracious provision, we spend our days learning about his great military might. His powerful army stands against the enemy's schemes taking place outside the great walls of the province. Battles are won and not fought within these provincial walls."

He gave Daisy a moment to reflect on his words, and then he proceeded, "Everyone in Niv lives and works in peace. This place has been built for our good pleasure and to bring joy to the King. You'll find no harm in learning or residing in Niv. The King's purpose has been set in motion and we get to participate in the future developments of furthering his plan."

"But Spotty mentioned the Sly One and..."

Again the sergeant interrupted Daisy, "The Sly One remains powerless within the province and no doubt you have encountered some of his tactics on your journey. It is only because the King has granted him some time that he even permits him an occasional romp into the province. This sly creature can attempt to scheme and mess things up for the visitors, but he's a useless, pitiful thing. One day when the time comes, we won't be seeing the likes of him anymore."

"Wow," uttered Daisy.

He continued, "Haven't you ever heard the saying, 'what you feed grows and what you starve dies'?" As he spoke the Zooker's family motto he had Daisy's full attention.

Then he said, "The Sly One can only make short visits into the province at a time; otherwise he would starve to death. He is unable to find sustenance or food to his liking within the province. This creature is known as the Sly One for various reasons. For one, he is the author of all confusion; and confusion does not exist within Niv. He is also known as the father of all lies; and those who reside in Niv have nothing to lie about. This creature thrives on corruption, as he is intent on killing, stealing, and destroying everything. Anything of that nature could not ever live, or remain within the province. Since the Sly One consists of and eats only rotten fruit, he is a shriveled-up being without a healthy thought and void of any sense of wholesomeness. He is a starved creature, without fur to keep him warm, without a heart to pump his platelets blood, and a set of lungs so full of holes due to rot that he can't even hold his breath. As I said, he would starve to death if he tried to make Niv his home, since nothing grows in the province to sustain his lousy appetite. Why, he's so useless that his state of being could be likened to a burned-out light bulb, a wet pack of matches, a moldy bale of hay, or an empty can of gas—all destined for the trash with nothing inside save maybe a putrid vapor. One day he will push his luck too far and get way too close. Why, all it would take is just one little spark from the King and poof—he'd be a goner. He's a real deadbeat if you ask me."

Daisy shuddered listening to his descriptive discourse accompanied with the metaphors about this wretched creature. She stored this information into her memory bank to pencil it later into the pink notebook.

Then the sergeant said, "To answer your concern about fences, those living in the province have made a decision about what side of the fence they want to be on, and therefore fences aren't a necessity here."

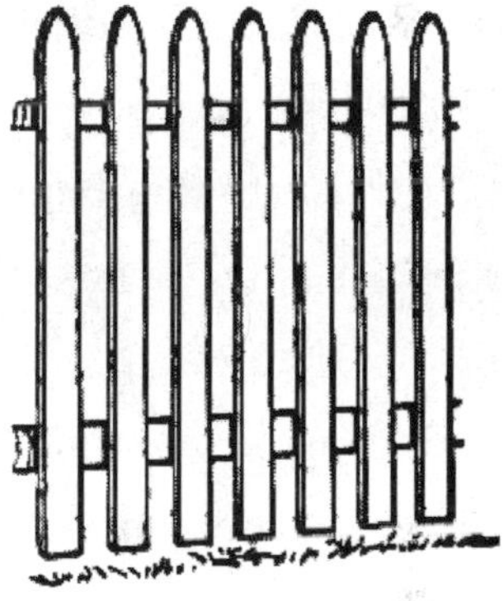

"Really," said Daisy.

He asked, "Have you made a decision in your life about what side of the fence you want to be on?"

Daisy shrugged her shoulders in response to his question.

She began contemplating what he said. She had never thought about fences being a sign of one having made a decision. As a journalist, words were her specialty. She considered the word "fence-sitting" as they pedaled along the road. Pondering the area of commitment, she knew she had been and continued sitting on the fence.

Since she became quiet again he asked, "Are you mulling over the idea about fence sitting?"

"Yes, I am," answered Daisy, saying, "My one main decision and commitment in life has been to make lots of money."

"How has that worked out for you?" he asked.

"I'm finding that making more money hasn't paid the price for the lack of commitment I have demonstrated in many areas of my life," she said.

"Ouch," replied the sergeant.

With that comment, the two stopped speaking for a while as the comrades piped another old tune.

Daisy rode along and did some soul searching. This fence-sitting idea pricked at her heart. She thought of herself as a bright, young over-achiever with a free spirit, and she sought to keep moral issues at bay for fear of becoming bogged down and hemmed in. Seeing another herd of animals roam free, she wondered if freedom came with staying in or outside the fence. Since arriving in Niv, all these lessons had made her take note of how she had been living her life. Without need of the sun, this place had a way of shedding new light on everyday life.

Daisy asked the sergeant, "When did you make up your mind which side of the fence you wanted to be on?"

"During my final year of high school before leaving for the army," answered the sergeant.

His answer brought Paul to mind. She could tell he had made up his mind about fence-sitting issues. He had shared his beliefs with her. She thought he limited himself and that his beliefs stifled his life, but now she saw his confidence, peace, determination, and strength. She realized Paul had been free to make choices without fear. His life demonstrated this to her all the time. She wanted this freedom too. Paul had made choices, and whatever those choices were brought about an obvious inner peace, a freedom, and an unyielding strength. With this solidified in her mind she pedaled along as these military men led her to the city.

Once again, she planned to journal in her notebook and figure out where she stood on the choices she had made and the direction she wanted her life to take. She checked under her shirt for her notebook and in her back pocket for the yellow number-two pencil. Since these were the only two items she could claim ownership for while touring Niv, she was determined not to lose them.

Spotty kept his vigil behind the group, flying overhead and keeping an eye out for the Sly One. He had become tired of the creature's antics and looked forward to getting to the city.

Chapter Sixteen:

A MOTHER'S INSTINCT

Ted Strain went to the trauma center to check on Ms. Zookes' condition. To avoid negative press, she had been placed in a private room at the insistence of the Hannah and Rhutkers JC Publishing Company. Since her accident occurred on company time and property, they were liable for her medical expenditures.

Strain and the human resource manager reviewed the company's policy outlining the ramifications and regulations set up for an employee injured on the job. He also met with the company's legal team and had conducted two meetings with the firm's medical insurance agency. He maintained a commandeering attitude, double-checking that the company adhered to its medical responsibilities.

Daisy's mother, Martha, met Mr. Strain in the trauma center foyer. She appreciated his visit to see her daughter. She overheard him and her husband discussing the company's medical policy and hospital stay information. During a prior telephone conversation, Daisy had mentioned Strain as being a real stickler at work; now Martha witnessed this negative quality of his working in her daughter's favor.

Martha walked back to Daisy's room and saw a large bouquet of flowers from the publishing company on the credenza. She assumed Mr. Strain had dropped them off earlier before she ran into him in the foyer. When she said goodbye to him just now, he stated he had to go back to the office. She watered the other arrangements of flowers from friends, including a vase of roses from Paul Thornchen. As a mother and wife, she could tell Paul's feelings and intentions ran deep for her daughter. Jonathan and her discussed this in their hotel room and neither disputed this fact.

Placed next to the roses, Darla's card read Get Well Soon attached to a cute teddy bear. As Martha surveyed these items, her heart began to ache for her lifeless daughter stuck in a coma between two worlds.

The doctor came into the room with Tulip and her husband. Jonathan told the doctor, "Teressa, Paul, and her mother and I have been keeping a constant vigil at her bedside."

"That's very good to hear, " said the doctor. The medical team believes your daughter's condition continues to show signs of improvement. Her bones, fractures, and bruises are beginning to heal. The swelling around the cranial area has also receded."

Martha listened to her husband respond, "Doctor, we had

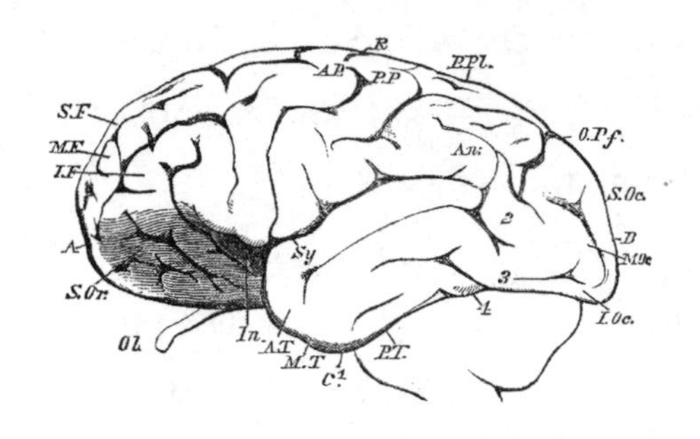

hoped for a favorable report such as this."

"Daisy's chart reveals that at various times her blood pressure rises, and the monitor indicates unusual spikes in brain activity. These findings mean she has been having some mental awareness—or it could mean she has been dreaming. The Staff is confident that in the days ahead she shall awaken from her coma."

Martha took hold of Jonathan's arm as he replied, "Martha and I prayed to hear these encouraging words."

The doctor chose not to share that the medical team thought it best Daisy remained in a comatose state, as it kept her very still while the crack to the cranial region healed. They had been of the opinion that the least amount of movement in the first week would be paramount to a long-term recovery. The team spoke in private about long-term brain damage with possible vision and speech impediments resulting from her cranial injury.

The doctor informed them, "Please understand, until she awakes from her coma, the medical staff can't know the full extent of her injuries. The brain has a way of reacting to certain head injuries, and the healing of cranial fractures and wounds react and behave differently from patient to patient."

Martha tightened her grip on Jonathan's sleeve as he patted her hand, "We understand, doctor, and we know you and your team are doing all that you can for Daisy."

The doctor nodded and then left the room. As he walked down the hall, he reasoned the family had enough to contend with and thought it unnecessary to alarm them any further until tests and time revealed more. He knew it continued to be a waiting game for both parties.

As Tulip sat next to Daisy's bedside, Jonathan spoke with Martha about his early morning telephone call to their business back in Pennsylvania, the T & D Nursery.

Jonathan said, "The apprentice, Gerald Bilkquist has everything running according to our expectations. Martha, we can waylay any fears you may have had; Gerald said no one at the nursery feels abandoned due to our absence. Our decision to hire Gerald has been a godsend, as you were right when you encouraged me to hire him. He has been an honest, hardworking man."

Tulip smiled, finding her parents' concern for others in the midst of their own stressful situation admirable. Jonathan kept quiet that he had spoken about his wife to Gerald. He had shared how overwrought she had been in dealing with their daughter's welfare. Gerald said he and his wife would be praying for their family.

Martha gave him a hug and said, "Dear, someone from the medical staff approached me this morning. He offered to prescribe me a sedative along with counseling if I felt the need. Now, I know you are worried about me Jonathan, but I am tougher than I may appear at the present time."

Jonathan said, "Martha, I'm sorry if I have upset you. This has been a difficult time for all of us. I spoke with the doctor and he thought a sedative might help, since you aren't sleeping very well these past few nights."

Martha stated, "I understand your concern, Dear. If I feel the need, I will speak with the doctor. Okay." She had no desire to take any medications, even though she felt weary. Plus she had been keeping her mothering instincts quiet, for she knew their daughter wasn't out of the woods yet.

Chapter Sixteen:

THE VINEYARD

"Thanks for letting me ride along with you," called Daisy, waving goodbye to the group of comrades.

Spotty bumped into some of his feathered friends at the city gate. They became engrossed in a conversation as the bicyclists pedaled away from the city's entrance towards the briefing center. Thus, he failed to see the Sly One camouflaged as a city dweller approach Daisy as she stood alone waving.

The Sly One nodded to her and said, "Hello."

Daisy returned the greeting.

Wanting to engage her in small talk, he asked, "Did you bicycle your way to the city?"

Daisy turned to the harmless-looking fellow and said, "Well, not all the way. We walked most of the way." Turning her head in the direction of Spotty and his friends, she added, " My friend Spotty and I have been traveling the thoroughfare for days."

The Sly One peered in the owl's direction, saying, "Oh, I see." Then he fought to soften his voice saying, "You have a nice smile." Then he asked, "Are you from here?"

The compliment caught her off guard and she answered, "No, I'm from Indianapolis."

Then he stated, "Indianapolis. You must miss it very much. Does your family know where you are?"

Daisy lingered for a moment, thinking about her family and friends. She did miss them. She began to question her decision to stay in Niv.

He smiled as best as he could without sneering while he probed at her heart and toyed with her emotions. Causing her to doubt, he began his purpose of swaying her from entering the city.

"I could help you find a way back to them," he lied. "You could go home, today.

Maybe you have a pet that needs your attention?"

At the thought of her precious cat Aloewishish, she bit her lower lip and wanted to cry. Feelings of homesickness arose within her. Her plans began to wane as he disrupted her entrance into the city. Thoughts of doubt raced through her, "I should go back. My cat needs me. What am I doing here?"

The Sly One watched the range of emotions portrayed on her face. He knew if he could get her to focus on her feelings rather than on her mission, she would follow him and not enter the city. With each question he posed to Daisy, he could see a longing within her eyes to go back. He utilized this last chance, for once she entered the walled city she would be out of his reach and grasp.

Spotty looked over from his group of friends and recognized the Sly One. He darted over to Daisy and faced the Sly One demanding, "What business do you have with us in Niv? Go away I tell you!"

Shocked at Spotty's outburst, Daisy reprimanded him for it. But when she saw the glint in the Sly One's eyes; and then his smile turned into a smirk it sent a chill through her body.

The Sly One responded in a deep guttural voice, "My deeds are none of your concern."

"Your deeds," said Spotty, "aren't of anyone's concern, except yours and yours alone; so keep them to yourself. Go back from where you came and leave us alone. You, selfish creature, are not welcome here!"

The Sly One's appearance changed to a disgusting figure. He turned away in a huff, revealing a hunched back and unkempt greasy hair. He made swift, jerky movements as he made his way down the road away from the city gates.

"And good riddance!" called Spotty after him.

Astonished at Spotty's boldness, Daisy thanked him for coming between her and the horrible creature. She knew now that Spotty hadn't only been her tour guide, but he had also acted as her protector.

Satisfied and relieved Spotty said, "Now, we shall have no more interruptions from the Sly One."

"He's the creature you told me about?"

"Yes," answered spotty, "that's him."

"He sure made himself sound like a caring and concerned individual. If I had known, I would have never spoken to him. Honest, Spotty."

"Don't trouble yourself, Daisy. He's not permitted beyond the city gates. Now, let's get on with our journey."

Daisy took one more look back to the Thoroughfare and noticed that the creature had left the road hobbling through an open field. She became glad knowing that he could not come into the City of Niv. The thought of seeing him again gave her the creeps.

Spotty and Daisy stood before the City Gate. A posted sign read, All Visitors Must Proceed to the Vineyard to Obtain a Visitor's Pass. A bold arrow pointed the way. They followed a narrow grapevine path outside the city's wall to the vineyard's visitor's station.

The station's simple wooden structure had a large beamed front porch and a single door. A small painted sign in a window read, Please, Come In. The scene reminded Daisy of a picture postcard of the wine country in Southern California.

Before they entered the visitor's station, Spotty explained to her about the visitor's pass. He said, "Upon entering the city of Niv, all visitors have to get a VEESA pass. Once inside the city, a visitor without a pass can have an adverse skin reaction due to the nearness of the energy source of light generated from the city's center, which is the palace. Perhaps you remember our talk about skynthesis and photosynthesis and where this process obtained its source of light? You will be issued a visitor's pass upon completion of the proper applications at the Vineyard."

"Okay, I think I understand. You know, visas are issued to visitors in the States too," said Daisy.

Spotty clarified, "This is a VEESA pass. It stands for "Vineyards Exemplary Eternal Skin Application."

"Okay, whatever," commented Daisy. Then she asked, "But will it cause discomfort or something unusual?"

Spotty chuckled as they entered the station saying, "It's similar to a spa treatment: just relax and enjoy yourself."

An attendant directed them into separate areas. As Daisy disrobed for the spa treatment, she thought about how out of the ordinary and yet how vaguely similar things tended to be in Niv. This included obtaining a visa, or VEESA. She listened to Spotty's assurances and complied with the vineyard attendant's instruction

She changed into a white robe the attendant provided for her. The attendant directed her into the open spa area. Daisy enjoyed the lavish creams and ointments applied to her skin. After a thorough massage, she took a dip in a sparkling pool. Upon drying with a soft towel, she laid on a warm square block of smooth sandstone while oils were applied to her skin. Daisy thought, "This is the best spa treatment I have ever experienced."

The attendant answered her questions about the creams and ointments, saying, "They are made from the grapes and wine solutions produced at the vineyard."

Afterward, she escorted Daisy into a small area to lounge while soft music played in the background. On a table lay an assortment of goodies. The attendant served her a glass of the vineyard's tasty wine. Daisy rested on a lounge chair. Her pink notebook and the yellow number-two pencil lay on a small stand next to her chair. Reclining, she cast a casual glance through the sliding glass door. She saw Spotty enjoying a birdbath extravaganza with other feathered friends singing and chirping away. A delicious scene of grapevines and beautiful figurines adorned the courtyard where the birds fluttered and bathed.

As she drank the exquisite glass of wine, her vision improved. She noticed she could recognize distant items. Under normal circumstances she would have had to strain to see so far away. The ointments and creams had left Daisy's skin feeling like a newborn baby.

Finding this perfect time to catch up on journaling, she penciled in the latest news. She pulled from her memory all the things since her last entry. Penciling away, she wrote how she felt new - not only on the outside -

but also from the inside out. Finished with journaling the vineyard's spa treatment and feeling renewed, she looked forward to the excursion into the city.

Once back at the station's front desk, the attendant issued Daisy the visitor's pass inscribed with the word VEESA. The attendant explained, "The twelve small precious stones strung on the cord signify the city's wall and its foundation. The gems are jasper, sapphire, chalcedony, emerald, sardonyx, carnelian, chrysolite, beryl, topaz, chrysoprase, jacinth, and amethyst. Please wear the pass at all times around your neck while in the city."

Daisy thanked her for her generosity. She met up with Spotty who waited for her on the front porch. The time had come for them to enter the gates and travel into the city.

Chapter Fifteen:

A WALK DOWN MEMORY LANE

With her visitor pass in place and Spotty hovering low near her shoulders, Daisy entered the great city of Niv.

"The massive gates stand fifteen feet high and they remain open for the citizens to come and go as they please," explained Spotty.

Fully garbed and adorned with ribbons, two sentries stood posted inside the gate. "Their general orders," said Spotty, "are to greet visitors, provide directions, distribute informational pamphlets, and to accommodate dignitaries. The sentries have an official title of the Provincial Salutatory Guard."

Daisy felt humbled in the presence of the uniformed, unarmed sentries who commanded respect.

Spotty said, "The sentries adhere to the King's general orders and follow a firm set of governing rules. The décor on their uniforms shows the royal honor and leadership bestowed upon them. Being commissioned as a sentry for the city is considered a great privilege."

Daisy studied a brochure a sentry had placed in her hand. It announced the upcoming "Endurance Games" to be held the day after tomorrow at the Grand Colossal Stadium.

Overjoyed with this news, Spotty exclaimed, "Hooray. We have arrived in time to attend one of the Colossal Endurance Games. The games are a grand event; thousands will be in attendance, including the King. The Palace sponsors a celebration after the game in honor of all the teams and is open to visitors. This will provide a convenient opportunity for you to meet with the King." Spotty chatted on in excitement about the upcoming endurance game.

After encountering the sentries, the two made their way through several groups congregating inside the gate area. Several different nationalities huddled together, each speaking their own language. Daisy listened as the multi-lingual sentries spoke with one group after another.

Citizens of the province provided samplings of finger foods from baskets. A Middle Eastern man served a warm drink from a contraption he carried on his back. He provided a small glass and poured the liquid through a funnel protruding over his shoulder. Daisy waved her hand to say, "No thank you," as she did not want to eat or drink anything at the moment.

Anticipation mounted within her, as she kept moving through the crowd to get her first glimpse of the city. She felt it paramount to view the city, as though it would answer some unknown question deep within her. Warmed by the welcome, her expectation compelled her forward through the crowd.

Once free of the crowd, she spied a street sign reading New Beginnings Lane. Spotty ushered her onto the lane. The lane curved to the right and wound up an embankment onto Cordo Boulevard. Catching her breath, Daisy crested the embankment as the city came into view.

She had to shield her eyes with her hand as bright rays emanated from the King's palace, illuminating the entire region. She compared it to the rising of the morning sun. Her heart leapt and she had to restrain herself from crying. Why the tears? She could only speculate. Daisy and Spotty stood for a long time beholding the sight of the city of Niv.

Silently they took in the view, contemplating its grandeur.

Breaking the silence, Spotty said, "I have been here a dozen times, but the view is new each time I return."

Turning toward the east, Daisy saw a cascading waterfall jetting out from the city's massive rock wall. Remembering the vineyard lay behind the wall, she wondered where this mammoth source of mystery water stemmed from. She hadn't seen a stream near the vineyard's visitor's station. The water flowed into a river after bursting forth from the wall. This river ran towards the center of the city, winding its way to the right and then back to the left, bridged by Cordo Boulevard. This boulevard led straight through the heart of the city and to the King's palace. The city's inescapable beauty held her attention.

Alive with vibrant colors, this city looked as though its designer had dipped his brush into a bucket filled with peace, and had splashed the color of peace all over the canvas Daisy and Spotty viewed. An intoxicating aroma of love permeated the air; with every breath her lungs captured this love.

Daisy stood engulfed with feelings of coming home. The scene's majestic view reminded her of her first glimpse of the Grand Canyon, along with the sunset over the ocean. The fresh air tingled as after a spring rain, and the scene reflected purity representative of an early morning snowfall. Glad to have made it to the city, she savored the flavors, which she likened to a fresh-picked apple on a Pennsylvania autumn day.

Once again, a sign appeared out of nowhere. She read: "Welcome to Niv—a place to call home. You will find a place to hang your hat on the hook that will never let it fall. Rest assured my friend, you'll discover the faucets don't leak, the tires never go flat, and the river stays on course. The dentist's office is a place to smile. The lawyer's office is open for citizens to mitigate instead of litigate. The tax office pays a refund without even filing a return. The caretaker has retired. Wall Street is just that—a walled street with a bell to ring, proclaiming prosperity. You will be glad to know this is the only large commercial sign existing within the city. Be of good cheer, as all modes of telecommunication are wireless and cable-free; you are in charge of the remote. A team spirit exists within; therefore, no one sits on the bench unless he or she wants to. Remember to work hard, to play hard, and to enjoy each other's company. Only one season is recognized on the provincial calendar, and that is the In – Season. The fruit remains ripe and ready for harvesting. The favorable climate conditions allow for all types of sports and activities, adding zest to your innermost being. The individual fashion statements represent all the cultures of the nations. The existing government is pre-established, pre-ordained, and predestined —any suggestions can be brought to the attention of the city's local council located on Progress Corner. Welcome home, my friend, and enjoy your neighbor. You alone are the melody of my heart. Signed, the King of Niv"

Glancing back toward the crowd at the gate, Daisy speculated that these people were making their way into the city to become a part of some incomprehensible plan.

Still standing on the mound at the t-intersection of New Beginnings Lane and Cordo Boulevard, she became more determined to meet with the King—uncertain of what lay ahead. Her goal to help Spotty with his endangered species report and her adventure story note-taking had now become secondary. At this t-intersection, her plans seemed to dim in the light of the palace and the splendor of the city.

She strolled over to the waterfalls and sat on a stone close to the water's edge. Watching the water gush forth from the city's gigantic rock wall, she took the yellow number-two pencil and wrote, describing her first view of the city. A mist sprayed her in the face near the falls. Her eyes scanned the water as an all-too-familiar voice became audible, and yet she saw no one.

Back at the trauma center, Tulip came alone into Daisy's private room. On this particular day, Tulip nerves became unglued. She had been having a tough time keeping her emotions in check with the mounting distress of seeing her best friend and sister lie so still. Plus, her heart carried the heavy weight of seeing her mother's saddened face daily. Tulip sipped ice water from a hospital-issued, white styrofoam cup she had picked up at the cafeteria. Remembering the doctor's orders to avoid moving Daisy, she wondered if splashing some ice water onto her sister's face could somehow trigger her comatose senses to awaken.

Tulip sat next to Daisy and began to splash a light spray of ice water with her fingers. She started to tell Daisy about memorable times they experienced as youngsters in their home in Pennsylvania.

She said, "Daisy, remember the time we took Mom and Dad's car for a joy ride down the street? We weren't even old enough to drive." Tulip laughed and continued, "When we pulled back into the driveway we both ducked our heads in a futile effort to hide, just in case our parents had returned home." She shook her head and said, "It was silly of us to think that they wouldn't see the car driving down our own driveway." She laughed again and said, "Boy, what a predicament as we stood before Mom and Dad, who wanted an explanation. All we could say was, it looked like fun. It seemed like the best answer at the time, especially facing our parents' discipline. We were frightened of their discipline and our parents were thankful we weren't in an accident or anything like that. You and I spoke and laughed for weeks about this exploit. Remember Daisy?"

After a short pause she said, "And remember the time Daisy, that our small municipal airport offered thirty-minute airplane rides for only five dollars on a Sunday? One time, you and I decided to skip church and took an airplane ride. We asked the pilot to fly over the vast fields of our father's nursery. Do you remember that?" She grinned at the memory and said, " We could see Daddy walking the fields after we asked the nice pilot to fly in low over the nursery. Daddy just kept waving and waving, not knowing that it was you and I in the low-flying airplane. We had such a good time and couldn't wait to tell him that we were the ones waving at him from the plane. We giggled with delight as we shared with him about our surprise airplane ride. Only later did we realize that Momma wouldn't be pleased once she figured we had skipped church. Oh how comical it all had been. We always had fun together."

Tulip went on about another childhood memory: "Remember all the times we would play our favorite music in the evening after we had finished doing the dinner dishes and our home work? It was always on a weeknight since we weren't permitted to go out on school nights. You and I would dance and talk for hours. Other times we would end up in our bedroom listening to cassette after cassette. Those were special times as we shared our secrets and innermost thoughts."

She leaned forward and cried as she poured out her memories, hoping that somehow the familiar words would ignite Daisy's senses and rouse her from the slumber that held her captive. Just as she splashed more water onto Daisy's face, a surprised nurse entered the room. She spoke kind words, seeing Tulip's feeble attempt to awaken her sister.

Moved with compassion, the nurse said, "I can see your anguish for your sister. But her cranial area is still healing and to jar her awake prematurely could prove detrimental."

Seeing the pained look in Tulip's eyes, the nurse gave her a reassuring hug. Then the nurse said, "It is better that we leave nature take its course and remain patient during the healing process. The brain is a complex organ and the encephalogram (EEG) is recording plenty of brain activity. Her other vital signs have shown a positive progression with each passing day. Plus, all of the other injuries she sustained in the fall are on the mend. I would say to just give it time and your sister will be her old self again."

At that, the nurse took the cup of water from Tulip and

returned to her workstation assisting other patients.

Tulip remained sitting holding Daisy's hand saying, "Daisy, oh my little sister, Daisy," and then she cried once again.

Upon recognizing her voice at the water's edge, Daisy uttered her sister's name, "Tulip." The waterfall's mist sprayed her in the face and she became aware of Spotty staring at her.

"Well, are you finished daydreaming and are you ready to get a move on? " quizzed Spotty.

Daisy shrugged her shoulders and picked up her notebook and the yellow number-two pencil. They commenced walking onto Cordo Boulevard. After hearing Tulip's voice she became homesick for her family, her friends, and most of all Paul. She reasoned staying occupied could keep her from dwelling on her feelings. So she made her way into the city with Spotty at her side.

Chapter Nineteen:

BIBLIOTECCA PROVINCIATA

The manicured lined Cordo Boulevard ran its path through the center of the city absent of all motorized vehicles.

"Walking is the general mode of transportation used to get around the City," said Spotty.

Daisy saw a host of people going about their daily lives at the local shops and businesses in the midst of buildings of an impeccable design. Each building complemented the next in style, strength, and craftsmanship.

Some of the sidewalks moved forward like an escalator, so she took advantage of this mode of transportation.

Daisy said, "I want to first explore the city's grand library."

Spotty answered, "It is called The Bibliotecca Provinciata. We will stop there first."

They stood before the enormous structure spanning more than two city blocks. Its exterior walls were designed with white, pink, and gray marble with mammoth columns

and steps that led to an arched opening. Many patrons entered and exited the great library. Facing the building, Daisy leaned her head back to read the words etched over the opening: It Is Written.

Spotty pointed to a memorial on display in the landscaped grounds. Encased in glass, a tree stood about the size of an ordinary apple tree. However, Daisy did not recognize its primeval fruit. A plaque placed at the foot of the tree stated, Obedience is Better than Sacrifice.

"All kinds of trees grow in the forest," Spotty explained. "Some produce nuts; others produce berries or fruit, and some have only leaves. Even the birds know which fruit is good for food and which fruit to avoid. If we eat from the fruit of a tree which is not meant for food, then we become sick and die. I have learned it's a good idea to follow the rules."

"As a small child, my mother would read me a bedtime story about a couple who ate a piece of fruit from the wrong tree," Daisy said.

"And how did that story turn out?"

"Not too good," said Daisy. "The couple had to leave their happy way of life."

"Well, then would you say that obedience would have been better for this couple?"

Before Daisy could answer, Spotty directed her attention back to the library.

"You go ahead and browse the library. We can meet back up in an hour or so. Okay?"

Daisy agreed. She had wanted time alone to research some information within the library. Entering the building, the reception area consisted of an open-air circular colonnade with tall marble columns. She could see her reflection in the luster of the polished wooden floor. Mosaic tiled artwork covered the walls. In the adjoining rooms, windows at the top of the walls allowed plenty of natural light to shine through. A dual staircase led up to the upper floors and bookshelves lined the walls and corridors on the upper floors.

Various groups of people convened on the dark cherry wood benches cushioned with green velvety cushions throughout the expansive area discussing literature. Daisy noted all the volumes of ornate hard-covered books on the shelves, leading her to wonder how they kept the covers intact. She thought, "Maybe library patrons are prohibited from checking out books?"

Daisy walked over to the information counter. A receptionist named Annaleeza Zchean Boullair greeted her saying, "May I help locate something, Miss?"

"Yes please. This is my first time to this library. I want to research some information about the solar system, endangered species, and foreign lands. Could you help me locate these items?"

On the counter lay a large open white book with a list of first, middle, and last names. Daisy assumed it contained a list of library patrons. She noted the book's textured pages consisted of a special parchment and that the names were done in a gold script.

Seeing Daisy eyeing the book Ms. Boullair said, "This book contains the list of those granted permission to check out materials from the Bibliotecca Provinciata. Visitors may utilize this library but are unable to check out any books." She pointed to Daisy's VEESA pass.

"I see," said Daisy.

Ms. Boullair smiled and added, "But I can help you find what you are looking for and you may preview the information while visiting our Bibliotecca Provinciata."

With her pink notebook and yellow number-two pencil in hand, Daisy followed Ms. Boullair to the third floor. Ms. Boullair stated, "This is the science department. You can see a wonderful display of the planets and the solar system in the center of the room."

Daisy couldn't ascertain how the model of the planets, sun, moon, and stars remained suspended within the middle of the room. The librarian told her how to find the other departments within the library. Daisy wrote this information within her notebook. Then Ms. Boullair said, "If you need anything I will be down at the front desk." And she left the room.

Daisy scoured the science department. She chose a few books to research and sat on a sofa near the solar exhibit. Scanning some articles about the sun, moon, and stars, she found it puzzling as it referred to these heavenly bodies in the past tense. She read fast, as she didn't want to spend the whole hour in one department. She located information detailing the process of skynthesis written by a Professor Marcu C. Hahn. That book had been written for someone with an Einstein brain and a superior intelligence. Unable to grasp the intellectual concepts, it became a chore for her to fathom the data, terms, and jargon used within the articles. Discouraged, but still fascinated by the solar system display, she decided to make her way to the zoology department.

She found the zoology department on the same floor as the science section, situated on the other side of the entryway's open rotunda. A collection of many life-like animals surrounded the entranceway to this department. Daisy thought, "Wow, the city's taxidermist does a fantastic job. These animals appear as though they could come alive at any moment." She found a bookshelf labeled endangered species. Once again, she became disconcerted to find them written in the past tense. She looked up information about the northern spotted owl. Feelings of distress overwhelmed her upon reading that Spotty's species had become extinct. Daisy questioned the dates within the research. She reasoned, questioning herself, "How did this information come to be recorded if the date hasn't yet transpired?" She decided to ask Spotty about these dates. Feeling befuddled, she walked back through the entranceway of the zoology department.

Daisy stopped when she saw a white, longhaired Persian cat among the taxidermist's display. She cried, "Aloewishish," as she reached toward the animal. Stroking the cat's fur, her head began to ache. The stuffed cat seemed to purr while she petted it. She missed Aloewishish. Her mind drifted as she wandered if Darla had been tending to her cat.

Darla arrived at Daisy's apartment to take care of Aloewishish. She had just left Tulip at the hospital, while Paul acted as chauffer for the parents. Being day three of Daisy's ordeal, she, Tulip, and Paul had spent a considerable amount of time together. In sync with one another, they found it easy to communicate within their new friendship

Earlier today, Darla had sat across Strain's large glass top, mahogany desk, adorned with peculiar artifacts from around the world. She had been summoned to his office for a meeting.

Now in Daisy's apartment, Darla sat stroking the cat's fur. She replayed the conversation between her and Strain.

Strain: "Ms. Firkens, I have made a decision about the story Ms. Zookes is working on."

Darla: "Do you mean the adventure story?"

Strain: "Yes. You will need to set aside your daily tasks and focus on this project. In the meantime, I have assigned your work to someone else. This story has less than a six-week deadline. I expect you to keep the story on target."

Darla: "Okay, I understand sir. I have been toying with an idea; perhaps it could work into an adventure story."

Strain: "Let's hear it."

Darla shared the information she had been accumulating about the plight of wild cats. She bent Strain's ear expressing the challenges the wild cats face with endangerment and extinction. Darla concluded, "I think it would make a good premise for an adventure story."

Strain: "Sounds interesting enough. Put it together and I'll look it over. I told Ms. Davenport we'd have an adventure story for her magazine, and I aim to keep my end of the bargain."

Darla added, "I can meet the challenge. But once Daisy is back to work, I would want it to remain her project."

Strain said, "Upon Ms. Zooke's return, you can finish the project together."

Both he and Darla counted on Daisy's recovery, Strain for personal reasons and Darla because she cared so very much for her good friend.

Darla commenced working on the project, utilizing the material from Daisy's *Cats* magazine. She believed most young readers would find a book about wild cats interesting. Putting her plan into action, she continued researching wild cat activity throughout the world. In her research she came across various information concerning many endangered species.

She made a list of what the research stated led to the wild cat's endangerment: loss of habitat due to clear cutting, new housing developments being built, humans encroaching on the animals' hunting grounds, and an excess of cats being over-hunted due to greed. All of these factors had had a huge impact on the future of the cats and the places left to roam for their natural habitats.

As she accumulated and researched about the wild cats' predicament, Darla became alarmed about the environment. Eager to explore a new area of study, she set about her task with fervor. The more information she researched and uncovered, the more her concern grew for the environment and the animals. Anxious to share her findings with Daisy, she wished for her friend to awaken from the coma. Certain Daisy would be interested, Darla looked forward to working on the project together. Plus, she knew that if anyone could write an adventure story from someone else's research, Daisy could.

Aloewishish jumped from her lap, and Darla set about watering Daisy's plants.

Shifting her thoughts from the cat, Daisy headed to the geographical center located on the second floor. She planned to overview some maps tracing the province of Niv to determine which continent could claim its dominion. As someone who enjoyed traveling, she found the study about other countries and cultures fascinating. An open book on a sectional sofa drew her attention. She sat down and began reading. She read an overview about traveling throughout foreign lands and what one could expect. A slogan at the top of the first page read, "Remember, the only thing foreign in a foreign country is you—the visitor!" Daisy chuckled. She had never thought about being the foreigner. The province had been full of peculiarities and different people. No one seemed surprised at the things she had encountered on her journey through the province. Everyone she met appeared right at home. If anything had been of a foreign nature within the province, it had been her. Everyone else belonged here. Then she thought, "That is, everyone but the Sly One. Yuck, just the thought of him makes me shiver."

Setting the book down, she went in search of the map drawers and found them along one of the walls. She looked over some of the maps. She recognized most of the jurisdictions of the states, counties, and continents. One map had a clear overlay attached outlining many of the continents. This showed where the oceans had overstepped their boundaries with another futuristic date notation. She thought it odd for someone to have drawn the maps with these markings.

She found a map of the province of Niv. Excited at first, she then became discouraged, as the map did not specify any neighboring lands or bordering countries. The map only outlined the city's streets and the outlying province. This information provided little help other than a quick overview of the city. She made some notes within her notebook about areas to visit in the city of Niv. She had planned to sightsee first and then go meet with the king. Meeting with the King became top on her list, whether Spotty wanted to attend the big sports game at the stadium or not.

Unsure how to process the information from her findings, Daisy strode back down the staircase. She had promised to meet Spotty at the library's entrance. Ms. Boullair nodded goodbye to her as she exited the doorway. Stepping outside and onto the steps, Daisy heard someone calling her name. Her friend Roni waved to her as she exited the library. Glad to see her friend again, she ran over to greet her. Seeing Roni again, made Daisy feel more welcome and less anxious to be back with her family and friends. The two women spoke to one another like old friends.

Daisy asked, "Where are Chancy, Chi, and Candrise?"

Roni said, "They're at the movie theater watching an educational film about the construction of the Great Wall of China. Some Chinese men and women who were forced to work on the wall produced the film as an educational, history tool."

Shaking her head in amazement, Daisy decided against her better judgment not to ask questions. With evening approaching, she looked forward to a rest.

Roni suggested, "Daisy, would you like to spend the evening at my house? I could take you on a tour of the city tomorrow and act as your tour guide."

It thrilled Roni to see Daisy again too. They both exclaimed, "It must have been our destiny." The two women chatted away. Daisy forgot about Spotty as he followed them to Roni's residence.

Chapter Twenty:

PUT IT ON MY TAB

Roni and the children lived on Academic Lane in an attractive, roomy home with plenty of open spaces for the children to interact. Daisy stayed in the upstairs guest bedroom, which was decorated with a touch of feminine décor. Spotty perched in the open window, and the two spoke until she fell asleep.

The next day, she awoke to a pleasing aroma of coffee and sweet toasted breads. Roni served the early morning meal on the back terrace. A picturesque setting of flowers and shrubs adorned the quaint backyard and terrace area. A light blue tablecloth and pastel dishware accentuated the breakfast display. Sitting on white wrought iron patio chairs, Roni and Daisy made small talk as they enjoyed the morning meal.

The children had eaten earlier and busied themselves with morning activities. Daisy could see Spotty and Chancy occupied in the far corner of the yard.

Candrise approached the two women and said, "Good

morning Daisy. Did Mommy tell you about the picnic in the park today?"

"Good morning," said Daisy. "What about the picnic in the park?"

"Oh, I almost forgot," said Roni. "The Fourth will be celebrated in the park today. The city council sponsors the event. I had planned for us to spend the early part of the day strolling about the city. After that, we can go to the market center and purchase picnic items."

"Sounds good to me," said Daisy.

With breakfast completed, the two women headed onto Academic Lane. They stopped at the Thesauri University located down the street. Roni wanted to speak with one of the professors.

Professor Emorej Egroeg Zingher greeted them as they entered his classroom. His beautiful wife Esther and he had been reviewing a multi-lingual syllabus for the upcoming classes. Both he and his wife taught a range of languages at the university. Taking a break from the syllabus review, they provided the two ladies with a short tour of the university.

Professor Zingher said, "The Thesauri University offers a variety of courses. Our primary focus of study centers on multi-lingual studies. The educational programs are well attended."

"Due to the scores of different nationalities and cultures represented throughout the province, all languages are available to study," explained Esther. "This includes a language native to Niv. Everyone within the province desires to learn this native language."

"I've heard most people speaking English within the province," said Daisy.

"All visitors hear their native tongue as the common dialect while visiting Niv," the Professor said. "The King affords this individualized language provision to all visitors of Niv. Otherwise, they would be unable to comprehend their visit."

"The official language used within the Province is called Hiroglifewigeleben," said Esther. "This eternal language originated from the King's spirit and will be forever spoken."

Daisy pulled out her journal and asked her to spell the word again. She had never heard of this language and doubted she would remember the exact pronunciation. Daisy thought, "This journal will be a life-saver, as I never expected to encounter so many different things." She continued to write as the professor and his wife spoke and provided the tour of the university.

"I appreciate the tour," Roni told the professor, "but I have come to renew my enrollment. I have been studying the Yoruba Language. This West African tonal language of the Yoruban area consists of three pitches: high, medium, and low. I learned that the pitch on the vowel determines the meaning of the word."

The professor interjected, "That is correct. Did you know

that a single word could have three different meanings, depending on the placement of the accent or the tone emphasis placed on the vowel?"

"It is a difficult language," said Roni, "but I am enjoying the class."

As they walked the halls of the university, the professors spoke about the students and the activities associated with provincial academic life. With the tour complete, Roni filed her renewal forms and the two women set about their day's adventure in the City.

Crossing Academic Lane, Roni and Daisy made a right onto Progress Street and then turned right again at Progress Corner. This put them on Cordo Boulevard and in front of the King's palatial lawns. Daisy stared at the phenomenal structure and palace gardens.

"Come on, Daisy," said Roni as she pulled her away from the palace. They strolled Cordo Boulevard taking in the sights. When they reached Merchants Allee, they made a left. The two women explored the shops and boutiques. Daisy found the city bustling with activity as they went from shop to shop, and business to business. She noticed most bystanders browsed and window-shopped, with very few purchases in hand. She thought, "It resembles more of a meet and greet party than an actual city business day, because many of the pedestrians sit socializing at the open-air cafes." She did observe a oneness among the citizens in their mannerisms and conversations.

At Market Square, Roni proceeded to purchase picnic items for the scheduled park outing.

After a few purchases Daisy asked, "Why haven't you had to use money to pay for any of these items? All I hear you say to the storekeeper at the time of purchase is, 'Put it on my tab, please.' In fact, that is all I hear anyone say when they buy an item."

"Within the Province," Roni explained, "debits or overdrafts are obsolete; and therefore, are not incurred. The provincial business accounting policy is set up to utilize only credits. Every citizen of Niv is issued an ongoing line of credit. One cannot earn the credit, trade it, or give it away. One simply receives credit and utilizes it for the common good and purposeful pleasure of residing within the province. The King had this system in mind. He bestows this gift of credit upon each and every citizen of the province. Each one uses the credit to tend to their daily lives. We all support our neighbors. This simple, uncomplicated accounting system has worked well. At the end of every day, the ledgers are tallied, the books are balanced, and the accountants are satisfied. The business exchange is stable and profitable."

"Whoa!" exclaimed Daisy, "How is that possible?"

"In his graciousness, the King loans the credit," Roni explained. "Each citizen shows their gratitude every time they access the credit system. However, the King does require one thing from us while utilizing his accounting system."

"And what's that?" Daisy asked.

Roni answered, "Interest."

"Aha, I knew there had to be a catch! Nobody pays your debts without expecting something, albeit interest, in return. Every bank and credit union in the world has a high interest rate with outrageous fees attached. How much interest does the King charge?" asked Daisy.

"In return for this provision, the required interest payment is summed up in taking time to recognize and thank the King. He desires that we grow in our relationship with him and to thank him for all that he does and continues to do on our behalf. He wants us to be interested in him and to remain debt-free from any and all entanglements. He also wants us to reach out to the visitors with the hopes of crediting them with the knowledge of his kindness and generosity. The bottom line for the King's accounting plan is to be free from debtors, have an interest in changing lives, live a balanced life, and enjoy the unaffordable peace that boggles the mind. The King tops it all off with his non-refundable love. Throughout the province, we give and share on account of what he has done and who he is. Would you like to invest into this type of accounting plan and begin an open line of credit with him, Daisy?" asked Roni.

Daisy looked at Roni holding the items they had purchased from the local merchants. She glanced around at all the different multi-national people milling about the market square. As usual, the topics of discussion centered on the King and matters of the heart. She wondered if Roni's utopian world of giving and sharing was real and could it sustain the complexity of life, as she knew it. She also wondered if Roni's world had only been a daydream with a penniless, happy ending.

Daisy grimaced, "Who ever heard of someone paying a debt they did not owe, and then ask for only gratitude in return?"

Roni said in return, "Welcome to Niv, Daisy."

Daisy shrugged her shoulders; this place had a way of probing her heart, causing her to look deep within her heart and soul—an area of her being she did not care to let others trespass. For Daisy, money had been a strong motivating factor. She reasoned for her to change her way of thinking about financial security and monetary goals would take some time. She could see that Roni waited for a response.

After a momentary pause, Daisy responded, "Spotty told me that tomorrow a sporting event will be held at the colossal stadium, and after that, a team's visitor reception. He said I would have an opportunity to meet with the King. I tell you what, after I meet with the King, then l will let you know if I am interested."

"Sounds fair enough to me," replied Roni. "I plan to go to

the endurance game at the stadium too; we can sit together. However, I won't be able to accompany you to the team's visitor reception. The children and I have a previous engagement. We can meet after the reception to finish this discussion."

Daisy agreed.

With that resolved for now, the two friends joined arm in arm and headed back to Roni's house. The children and Spotty had waited for them to go to the Fourth celebration in the park.

Chapter Twenty One:

THE LONE STAR

Entering Sycamore-Fig Park, Spotty nestled in a tree near the orchestra's stage. He said, "I want to be close to the stage when the music commences for the festivities." He waved Daisy on and told her to have a good time with Roni and the children.

Enjoying the perfect picnic weather, Roni and Daisy spread out a couple of blankets and arranged their picnic items. Several other picnickers did the same as the orchestra set up and fine-tuned their instruments. The children took off for the playground.

Daisy said, "I'm glad we didn't have to travel far to get here. I'm bushed from all we did today."

"We did have a busy day so far, but I had fun. The walk along the river to get here topped off our sightseeing for the day, don't you think so, Daisy?"

"I did like walking along the river. By the way, what's the river called?"

Roni answered, "It's called The River, plain and simple. By the way, the Grand Colossal Stadium is just six blocks from here. Tomorrow, we will watch the endurance games at the stadium."

Daisy said, "Sounds good to me. But for now, let's eat something. I'm famished." She became hungry seeing the other picnickers indulging in their baskets of goodies all about the park.

In the festive atmosphere, the two women looked forward to the Fourth Celebration. Daisy looked towards the playground area and watched the children playing all sorts of games. The river bordered the western side of the park. Several people lounged by the water's edge and ate figs from the fruit trees.

Roni noticed Daisy looking towards the trees and mentioned, "Those are sycamore fig trees. The park derived its name from those trees. The figs are scrumptious."

After snacking on some food, Daisy and Roni rested on the colorful striped knit blankets they had spread out on the lawn. Chancy, Chi, and Candrise continued to play with the other children.

"I don't understand why there aren't any flags flying or other Fourth of July memorabilia on display within the park," said Daisy. "You did say this is the Fourth we are celebrating?"

"Oh Daisy, this isn't the Fourth of July. Today, the province will celebrate the Fourth Day and what transpired on that day. I should have explained this to you. The full name for the holiday is The Fourth Day Celebration, but we shorten it and simply call it 'The Fourth'. We celebrate with a day at the park with food, games, and music. Then in the evening, the sky changes from its lighter blue hue and turns into a navy blue shade. The King simulates this navy blue shading for one hour granting a vast display of heavenly bodies to become visible throughout the firmament. Soon, we will glimpse some signs and wonders. For you, this may not be anything new; but for those of us who have lived here a long time, it is a time to reflect and remember the sun, moon, and stars."

"Roni," said Daisy, "are you saying the sky will change its color, and we will see the stars shining and stuff like that?"

"Yes. The city council puts the program together and organizes the event, but it is the King who commands the simulation."

Daisy thought about what Roni said. She hadn't experienced nighttime since arriving in Niv. She remembered Spotty's earlier conversations about the sun being unnecessary within the province due to enough light and energy being generated from the city. She had witnessed first-hand how much light radiated from and within the area of the King's palace. She figured the simulation of nighttime would be a welcome sight. She missed seeing the sun, moon, and stars.

"The navy blue color filling the sky would be akin to a huge planetarium." Roni explained. "We will be viewing the stars, planets, constellations and other solar bodies."

Daisy had brought her pink notebook and the yellow number-two pencil along to do some journaling. Now, she planned to journal this evening's event.

The hungry children rejoined Roni and Daisy on the blankets. An hour later, an elder councilman stood near the orchestra announcing the King's edict, "Throughout the province, a navy-blue hue will be simulated within the sky for one hour. This simulation of color within the sky will be devoid of darkness; the sky will only have the appearance of a darker shade, thereby representing nighttime. The nighttime simulation is necessary to enhance the appearance of these great lights. This will give the effect of how they once existed. Every object in the sky will remain in a specified orbit and travel a predestined pathway. On the program tonight, we will see a visual projection of the planets, the sun, different moons and stars, the Milky Way, trailing comets, some asteroids mixed with meteorites, and other celestial bodies. The program will end with the appearance of the lone star. We invite everyone to sit back, relax, and enjoy the show."

Once the councilman finished, the orchestra minstrel, Matathias Mictheal J. Marconnico, commenced leading the symphony. They played a delicate flute serenade.

Suddenly, a powerful voice resonated throughout the province and declared, "Let a navy-blue hue appear and shade the firmament above!" At that instant the sky turned a navy blue shade and the stars shone in the sky. In unison the park dwellers made the sounds of oohs, and aahs.

As the orchestra played one symphonic oration after another, a mesmerizing mood fell upon the citizens and guests of Niv. The cosmos came alive in the evening sky and portrayed its beauty and splendor. More "oohs" and "aahs" could be heard among the park visitors as the show continued

During the hour-long show, Daisy remained suspended in time. She had a profound awareness of life going on and existing beyond her finite existence. Removed from her everyday world, she continued to view the projected display of the sun, moon, and stars. She could relate to the solar objects, but yet she remained separated from them. Life in Niv had brought about a disassociation of her everyday life. For a brief moment she thought she should be afraid, but instead she chose to embrace this enchanting opportunity and celebrate the cosmos, as she knew it.

Candrise sat next to Daisy. Every so often, she would point her tiny finger and express excitement of the wonder of the celestial bodies.

Daisy thought how often she had taken the nighttime sky for granted. Until missing them these past few evenings, she hadn't been aware how precious the stars had been to her. With her arm around Candrise, together they watched the beauty of these created and simulated astronomical spheres.

The music slowed as a full moon hung in place as a

deeper shade of navy blue engulfed the background. The moon's shape changed representing different times and seasons.

Daisy gasped at a spectacular view of the planets, noting the rings around Saturn and the many moons of Jupiter.

Then the music changed to the hunt as the great constellation of Orion the Hunter captured the sky. Candrise turned her head in toward Daisy's body as Orion became showered with meteorites. Haley's comet followed, bursting into the sky. The comet's trail sailed through outer space

An unexpected shooting star shot across the expanse. Daisy made a wish at the sight of the shooting star. Her wish became more of a prayer asking, "Please don't let these marvelous cosmic bodies become extinct." But she reasoned, "How could I stop the hands of time, and how could this show be taking place?" Gazing around, she noticed everyone enjoying the show. She wondered, "Why aren't they sad or concerned knowing the fact that these heavenly bodies will or have become extinct?" She shook her head as she thought these uncanny ideas. She said to herself, "Is Niv located in some other galaxy? Then Candrise squeezed and hugged her tight and Daisy went back to enjoying the show. Her days of journeying into Niv had taken her down many thought-provoking paths. This illuminating hour in the park became a picnic basket full of stargazing wonderment and unanswered astronomical questions.

The music played on and she treasured the nighttime scenes with a new appreciation. Daisy determined she would never let the wondrous beauty of the solar expanse escape her appreciation again.

She overheard the two boys conversing with Roni about the constellations. Sitting in the park on a blanket, Daisy knew this evening would remain forever etched in her mind, regardless if she wrote it in the notebook.

Accompanied by drums and cymbals, the orchestra's horn section trumpeted a crescendo at each spectacular starlit moment. For a split second, the sun lit up the sky. The onlookers had to blink fast and shield their eyes from its bright form. Then as quick as it came into view, it diminished and the expanse went back to the deep navy-blue hue, followed by more stars and constellations. Fascinating the crowd, the Aurora Borealis sprang into action pumping colors of swirling, gaseous designs. Captivated by the music and their glow, Daisy became engulfed by the forces radiating from the array of the northern lights.

As the hour came to a close, the navy-blue sky became a lighter hue while the orchestra continued to play a somber piece. A single star came into view. A solemn hush fell over the spectators. Daisy recognized a part of the holiday medley as '"Oh Holy Night." The star traveled across the sky and came to rest in the middle of the expanse. With the lone star standing still in its orbit, the orchestra finished the rendition with a bounding fervor.

Candrise whispered to Daisy, "It is the Lone Star."

"What do you mean, it's the lone star?"

Candrise explained, "Mommy told me about this star. She said this one star showed the way on the King's divine night. She said this star helped to direct some important men who had been looking for the baby King." Candrise looked knowingly into Daisy's eyes. Daisy nodded, acknowledging she knew the familiar story. Her parents had been intent on sharing it with both her and Tulip during their formative years.

She redirected her attention to the sky. The orchestra played on as the lone star lingered, becoming the highlight of the evening. This one solitary star brought more feeling and warmth than any of the other radiant stars. A deafening applause arose at this moment in the show, causing all to stand in awe of what this Lone Star represented.

The cosmic show ended along with the deep navy blue simulation. The color faded and the sky returned to light once again, with the Lone Star hanging in the expanse.

The councilman announced, "Per the King's edict, the Lone Star will remain in the hemisphere throughout the evening until morning."

As all the people settled onto their blankets, the crowd spoke late into the evening about the spectacular display of lights.

Daisy had been delighted at this opportunity to view the familiar and not-so- familiar evening lights. She marveled at her new sense of appreciation for the evening sky. She thought, "How will I explain this viewing of the solar system and how it affected me?" Yet she knew she needed to pen this experience into the pink notebook.

When all became quiet she wrote these words, "The heavens declare the beauty of the King, the work of his hands, his majestic work, his splendor." She further described the sky with its richer shade of navy blue. As she penned these two words, she thought of the navy blue suit she had worn to work the other day. Her hand began to shake as she gripped the yellow number-two pencil. Feeling as though she were falling, she spiraled, going down, down, down, until a heavy sleep forced her eyelids closed.

Chapter Twenty Two:

THE FLY OVER

The head nurse at the Indianapolis Trauma Center began her evening rounds. She entered Ms. Zooke's room and observed the unusual movements the patient made with her right hand. Upon a closer observation, she watched the comatose patient's eyelids flutter as her heart monitor registered a rapid heartbeat. Utilizing the in-house intercom system, she paged the physician on duty.

Dr. Kabintzol answered the page. He examined Daisy and took notice of the fluttering eyelids, but the movements of her right hand had ceased. The heart monitor continued to track a rapid heartbeat. He scribbled on her chart, ordering a series of tests for first thing the next morning and he instructed the nurse to get Ms. Zooke's parents on the phone.

"Jonathan," the doctor said, "this is Dr. Kabntzol. I have just been observing your daughter. I am happy to say that she is displaying some initial body movements. This could be a sign that she is emerging from the coma."

Jonathan answered, "That's good news, Doctor."

“Yes, this is very good news. I am ordering a short series of tests that I plan to oversee first thing in the morning. I would like you and your wife to be present for the results.”

“We’ll be there. Thank you Doctor.”

“See you here first thing then, and good night.”

Replacing the phone on its stand, Jonathan told Martha word for word what the doctor had said. They had been resting in their hotel suite, taking a much-needed break from their daughter’s hospital bedside. Martha knew that Paul and Tulip had decided to have a late dinner together to discuss the prospects of a prolonged comatose stay. She informed her husband, “This is the first time we have left Daisy’s bedside unattended. We need to telephone Tulip.”

Jonathan agreed and they telephoned Tulip’s cell phone sharing the good news. On the phone call, Tulip told her parents as soon as she finished eating, Paul would be driving her to the hospital. She would spend the night at her sister’s bedside.

The children and Roni had been packing their leftover picnic items. They watched in amusement as Spotty feather-dusted Daisy in the face with his right wing.

Daisy awoke with feathers strumming the left side of her face.

Spotty piped, “I’m glad you have decided to rejoin us Miss Daisy. We are waking you early, because we don’t wish to be late for the game.”

In a stupor, Daisy jumped to her feet trying to recall the

faces and place. Stretching and yawning she relaxed, saying, "Good morning. Thank you for waking me Spotty." Looking around the park she asked, "Say where is everyone?"

"The evening show has long since finished. Most of the spectators are heading to the grand colossal stadium to watch the game."

Daisy said, "Sorry about falling asleep on you. I hope I didn't put a damper on your evening, since we ended up staying the entire evening in the park."

Roni responded, "It is customary to spend the evening sleeping in the park after the Fourth celebration. Sleeping outside under the lone star has become a tradition within the province. The citizens have found it to be nice way to top off the Fourth celebration."

"Did you enjoy the stellar show and the music program last night," asked Spotty.

"Yes. I thought it was a remarkable show," said Daisy. "The planet exhibition, the lunar arrangements, and the orchestrated music were all spectacular. I am grateful you invited me."

"We're glad you came too," interjected Candrise who stood close to her mother's side looking up at Daisy.

Daisy smiled at Candrise, remembering how they had snuggled during the show.

The small group finished folding their blankets and packing their leftovers into the picnic basket. They made their way out of Sycamore-Fig Park. Daisy double-checked for her pink notebook and the yellow number-two pencil as the children ran ahead in the direction of the stadium.

"The grand colossal stadium is located a couple of blocks on the other side of the King's palace," said Roni. "We'll have to walk a few streets back over the bridge onto the Cordo Boulevard through the theater district." Once on the boulevard, they accessed the moving sidewalk toward the palatial lawns and took a right into the city's theater district.

"I'd like to visit a museum and stop at the theater when we have a chance."

"Perhaps tomorrow, Daisy, we could make time, if you'd like."

They passed a dance studio and an art gallery, which piqued Daisy's interest. Crossing three streets within the district, they made a left onto Sports Arena Way. The enormous grand colossal stadium came into view at the far end of the street. The structure encompassed several city blocks with its seating sections towering toward the sky.

Accessing the stadium at the street level placed them at the midway section of the stadium's seating area. The rows of seats ran as deep as they did high from this street entry point. Daisy held her breath, overcome with the enormity of the seating capacity.

"Due to the rectacletangular design of the stadium, one can view the playing field in its entirety from any seat in the stands," said Spotty.

Clueless to the meaning of rectacletangular, Daisy replied, "It's huge."

Spotty enlightened Daisy about the construction and layout of the sports arena, explaining, "the builders modeled the arena in a rectacletangular fashion. This is an ovaled, angled, rectangled, and tri-ocular, depth-perceptive shaped stadium. It seats four hundred and fifty thousand spectators. The structure stands seven stories high, and descends seven stories deep. The frame is made of a strong, durable, and lightweight material called Irotalnineym. This raw material is found only in the province."

Amazed at the keenness of her eyesight, Daisy had the ability to see the field at this great height. She speculated that the vineyards spa treatment coupled with the retacletangular design of the stadium improved her vision. She felt for the VEESA pass hanging around her neck as per the vineyard attendant's instructions.

Pointing to a row of seats on their right, Roni suggested, "Let's sit over there, shall we?" She directed the children and Daisy to the chosen seats.

"Excuse me ladies," said Spotty, "but I am going to sit with some of my friends to watch the game. I will catch up with you later."

The children giggled as Spotty flew high into the stands above the stadium's top row of seats. They watched him perch next to some friendly fowl buddies, then settled in to watch the pre-game activities.

A woman with long, beautiful hair approached Daisy. She said, "Hello and welcome to the games. My name is Jayska Podderick. I have a complimentary pair of multi-dimensional sunglasses along with an arena sports pamphlet for you."

"Thank you," said Daisy.

"The pamphlet outlines the field, explains the sequence of the game and its rules, and introduces the teams," said Jayska.

"What are the glasses for?"

"We provide all visitors a pair of multi-dimensional glasses to aid in viewing the fly-over during the opening ceremony."

Daisy took notice of others wearing the multi-dimensional glasses. Aside from their visitor's passes, the glasses identified them as visitors. The number of visitors surprised her.

Going on her way to hand out more pamphlets, Jayska called out, "Enjoy the game."

"Why don't you have to wear these special multi-dimensional glasses to view the flyover, Roni?"

"The King," said Roni, "bestows the capability to see, think, and to hear multi-dimensionally upon all the citizens of the province. Therefore, the children and I won't have any difficulty viewing all aspects of the game's fly-over. Please do wear the glasses, as you won't want to miss any part of it."

Before the pre-game events began, Roni previewed the endurance game pamphlet with Daisy. A picture showed the dimensions of the playing field with a length of one hundred meters long and a width of seventy meters.

"The field consists of two rows of three circles. Each circle has a diameter of thirty meters. A player will run against the grain within the revolving circuit of four complete circles." Roni pointed to the two starting positions outside the beginning circles. She continued saying, "The distance the player runs is the total track circumference of four circles. Each teams runner is faced with the challenge of running against the grain of the rotating track of the four circles. A member of a team begins his or her race at the starter's box."

Daisy said, "I don't see the circles rotating on the field right now."

"That's correct," said Roni. "When the players take their places on the field, then the track will begin to rotate. All teammates will commence running in place on sensor pads. Their effort of running in place slows the track's rotation speed. Once the track reaches a predetermined speed, a loud blast shoots forth from the center goal post's cylinder. This signals two runners to start running the track's course."

"Then do the teammates keep running in place?"

"Yes," said Roni. "The teammates must run in place the entire time, as the speed of the track is determined by the force exerted on each teammate's sensor pad. That's why it is called endurance. Each player endures prolonged running throughout the game until their teammate runs the track's circuit and reaches the goal box."

"This sounds like a game of pure exhaustion," said Daisy.

"The players are in great shape, but it does take a lot of strength and endurance to keep running in place to maintain a slower rotation of the moving cylindrical track. It is exciting to watch who will make it to the goal position first."

"This game sounds fun. How many points does one score for reaching the goal first."

Roni explained, "The teammate who reaches the goal box first earns three points, while second place earns two points. But, that is provided the runner makes it to the goal box without being tagged. Once at the goal box, the first and second place finishers will have an opportunity to score an additional extra goal kick point."

Daisy asked, "How does a player get tagged?"

"This is where the taggers come into play."

"The who?"

Roni repeated, "The taggers. They are an independent third team that competes against the two opposing teams. The tagger's sensor pads are located in the very center of each circle. They will run the circuit independently, opposing both teams."

"You mean there are three teams competing against each

other?"

"Well yes and no. The two teams competing today are the Blue Diamonds Squared and the Tri-Gems Cubed. The taggers will attempt to tag runners from both teams to earn their own points. The taggers are the fastest known individuals within the province and play this sport as a separate entity. Their goal is to earn points independently."

Then Roni added, "A square within each circle contains three taggers' positions. The four opposing players are positioned outside the taggers' square yet within the inner circle. The tagger's team casts lots prior to the game to decide which three of the four players they will chase and attempt to tag throughout the course of the game. Only the taggers know who has been chosen to be chased during the game."

"Do the Taggers run in place on sensor pads too."

"Yes. The taggers' sensors also affect the rotating speed of the track. The Taggers run in place to cause the circle to spin faster. They hope to slow down their opponents running the track in hopes to catch and tag them. A tagger will run with the grain of the rotating track when chasing a player. All three teams endure running in place throughout the game affecting the rotating speed of the moving track. It is a masterful game of endurance."

"But if a tagger runs with the grain and the opponent runs against the grain, wherein lies the sportsmanship?" asked Daisy.

"What makes it a fair game is that a tagger doesn't start chasing an opponent until his chosen opponent has reached the initial opening of the third circle. This gives the opponent a major head start. As soon as the opponent enters the third circle, the tagger proceeds to run with the directional turn of the rotating track and rapidly gains speed. Since the runner is so far ahead, this enables the tagger to catch up. However, once the tagger enters the final circle, the tagger must run against the grain in pursuit of the opponent. It is in this fourth circle that a tag can occur."

"How do we know if the tagger has officially tagged an opponent?"

"We'll know because a leaf will light up signifying a tag has occurred. See the leaves embedded on the circular track? If an opponent and a tagger step on a leaf simultaneously this results in a tag. The leaves illuminate if two runners contact the same leaf. But, both the tagger and the runner will continue onto the goal box, as all finish times are recorded. If the opponent is tagged, then the Tagger will earn the points and the tagged player forfeits his leg of the race."

"Who will we be rooting for today?" asked Daisy.

"Our seats determine which team we are to root for. We are sitting in the Blue Diamonds Squared section."

Daisy asked, "You mentioned a goal kick. What is that?"

Roni explained," Whoever gets to the goal box first, either the tagger or the opponent, gets to earn an additional point.

This is the second part of the scoring possibilities. It is called the goal kick point. The player or tagger will kick a ball between the center field's spinning goal post. The goal post is spinning very fast."

"Do you see the goal post in the center of the field? The goalpost point is a difficult shot to make. It is based on the speed of the spinning goal post, the timing and placement of the player's kick, and the torque or thrust placed on the ball by a player's kick. The players and taggers have practiced and studied this equation of physics pertaining to the goalpost kick. A marker on the ground registers the speed of the spinning goal post before the kick. If a tagger or opponent scores a goal, he or she earns an additional one point for their team."

Daisy head began to swim with all the information.

Roni laughed and said, "This is where you, the crowd, and I come into play. Under our feet are sensors too. We stomp our feet on the sensors during the goal kicking time. This affects the speed of the spinning goal post, accompanied with the teammates running in place again."

"You mean we participate in the game as well."

"Yes, that's right and it's a lot of fun. The fans want to slow down the spin of the goal post to help the kicker make a point for their team. It is so loud and exhilarating during this point of the game of endurance that hearing is almost impossible."

Daisy looked at Roni and said, "Unbelievable. Okay, let

me get this straight. The two opposing teams' objectives are to reach the goal first in order to score the most points, without getting tagged. They want to keep abreast of the taggers, since being tagged results in them forfeiting a chance to score any points. When a tagger tags a player, then the tagger earns the points, but all continue to race to the goal box to keep track of times. First place earns three points and second place earns two points. Then the opponent or tagger will get a chance to kick the ball between the spinning goal post to earn an additional extra point. Am I correct so far?"

"Yes."

"Is it possible for two taggers to reach the goal box first?"

Roni answered yes again.

Then Daisy stated, "And we are sitting in the Blue Diamond Square section. That is who we are rooting for and we get to stomp for them during the goal post kicking."

Roni said yes again adding, "I should point out that once each race is completed, the players and taggers change positions by moving one spot to their left, and change from circle to circle. This leads to every player occupying a different circle throughout the duration of the game. Once everyone has rotated on the field, the game commences once again. This rotation of players and taggers results in each circle having varying speeds, thus giving no circle or team an advantage. A total of twelve races will be run to complete the game."

THE BLUE DIAMONDS SQUARED

Richard the Brit
Theodor the Dane
Chris the American
Thadeus the Centurion
Taki the Greek
Luan the Albanian
Phaistos the Cretan
Titus the Roman
Chu the Eskimo
Marco the Italian
Warner the German
Abishai the Mighty Warrior

THE TRI-GEMS CUBED

Daiki the Japanese
Bagrat the Asian
Sashenka the Russian
Cyril the Slovakian
Geteye the Ethiopian
Sargon the Syrian
Sergio the Argentian
Sinuhe the Egyptian
Kohana the Sioux
Salamon the Hungarian
Clint the Texan
Milan the Croatian

THE TAGGERS

Yousef the Moroccan
Alemana the Hawaiian
Mataafa the Samoan
Jens the Icelander
Leon the Spartan
Pallaton the Indian
Jumoke the Nigerian
Hank the Canadian
Cordero the Spaniard
Goiridh the Scotsman
Hector the Trojan
Alejandro the Panamanian
Morani the Kenyan
Juan the Mexican
Tamarlane the Persian
Tochtli the Aztec
Mordechai the Hebrew
Yeghia the Armenian
Amadee the Frenchman
Min Ho the Korean
Bert the Australian
Johannes the Swiss
Klemens the Austrian
Gabir the Turk

As the band began to play, Daisy read a footnote in the listing of the team names. The note stated: All the teams consist of avid sportsmen, who have spent their lives competing, training, and disciplining in a desired sport. They excel in the area of physical fitness. The Blue Diamonds Squared and the Tri-Gems Cubed are multi-faceted sports-minded individuals, while the taggers are strictly runners. Upon becoming citizens of Niv, these sports-minded individuals have decided to continue in their love of sports. The game of endurance is a non-contact sport. However, it does require agility, speed, strength, and a competitive heart.

The band drummed louder drawing Daisy's attention to the field. Watching the teams enter the arena, Daisy could see the exceptional amity amongst all the teams mingling on the field. The sportsmen laughed and encouraged the crowd to cheer. Daisy realized that while she and Roni had been studying the sports pamphlet, the stadium had filled with spectators.

Daisy took note of a special boxed-in seating area across the stadium from where they sat. She asked Roni about the special booth.

"The King sits in this section to watch the games."

"Then at least I will get a chance to get a glimpse of him," said Daisy.

Daisy took note of the team's colorful array of ornamented robes. She said, "I haven't seen robes like these represented in a sporting arena."

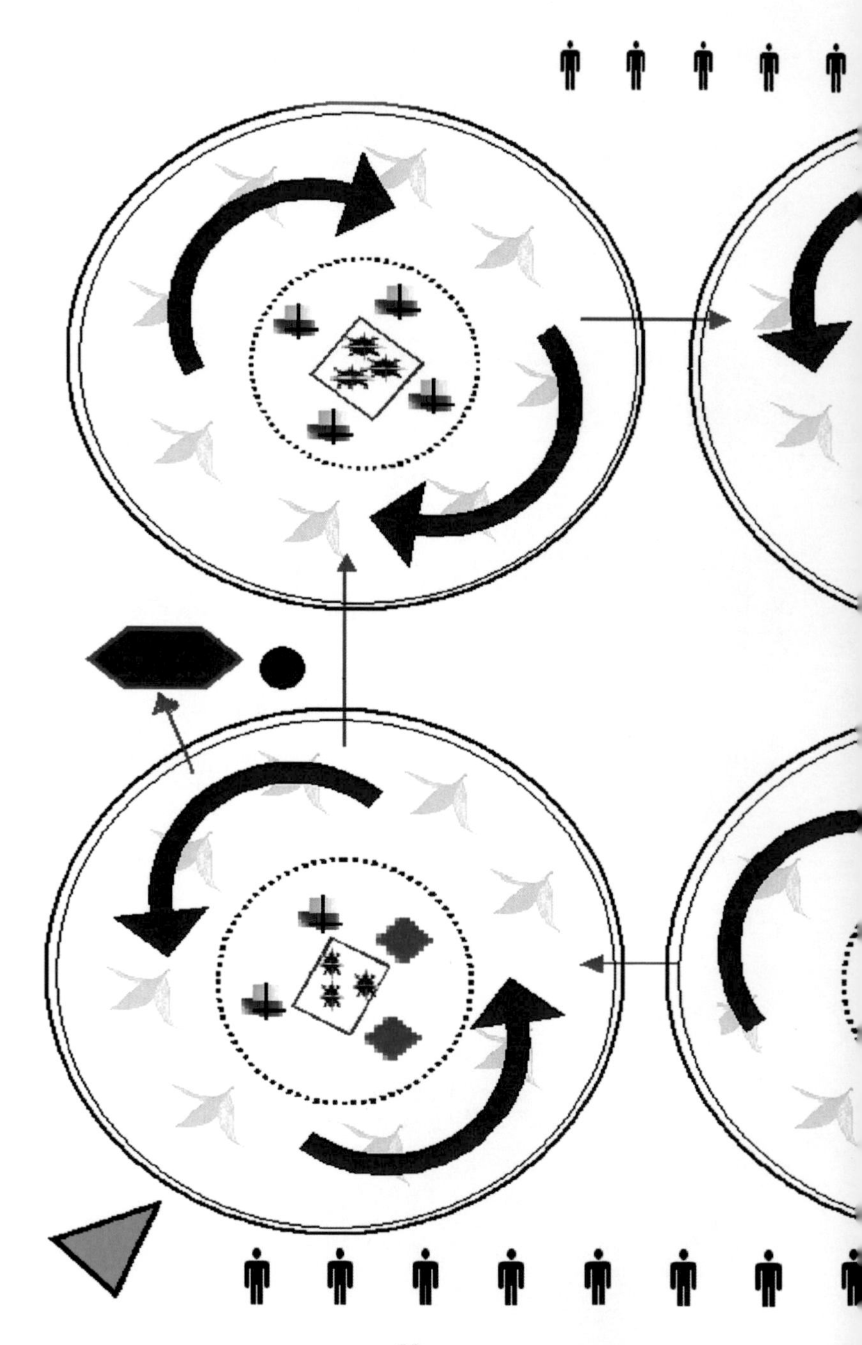

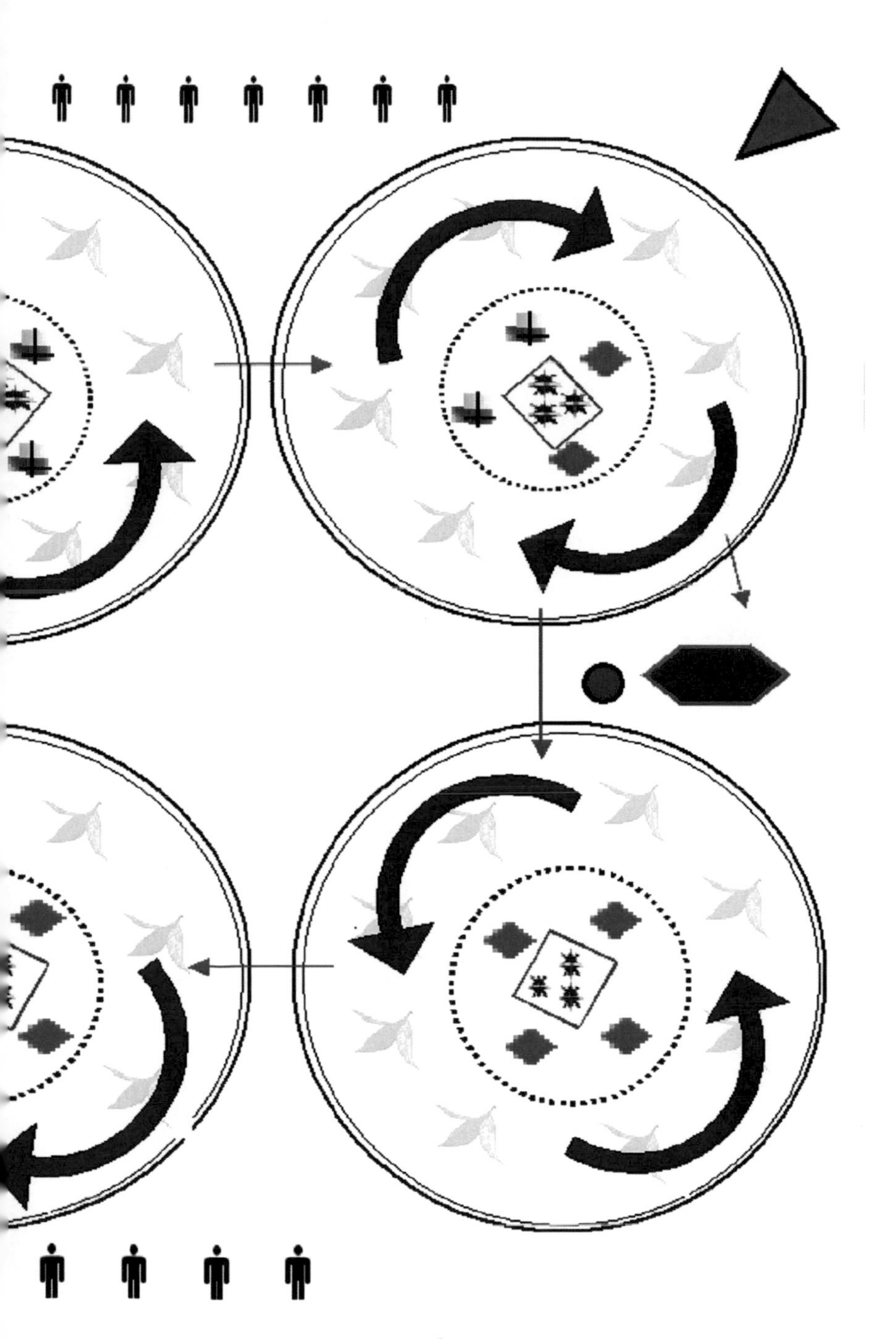

Roni said, "Their robes represent the country or culture of their nationality. Underneath the robe, the players wear a simple white jersey and white linen shorts with a silver seam. An emblem on the back of their jersey signifies their team by a blue diamond, a cubed gem, or a tri-colored asterisk. You can read each player's name on the back of the jersey."

"What's with their shoes? They look like bobby-socks."

Roni explained, "Their socks and shoes are made of one piece of off-white soft leather. It's a slip on sock-shoe with a cushioned support bottom. The outer sole has been designed to grip the track."

Daisy watched as the three teams formed two lines. A colorful mixture of cheerleaders entered the field and stood on the outer perimeter, inciting the crowd to cheer. The band kept playing amid the excitement. Once all three teams had lined up, everyone stood up and became quiet.

A drum roll sounded and everyone in unison turned toward the field's center gate. The King made his way onto the field, accompanied by a group of provincial dignitaries. The King and the dignitaries walked between the lined teammates and the players knelt, paying homage to their King.

Daisy could see the King's long

white robe and his inlaid gold belt. He wore a navy blue sash draped over his shoulders; and a pair of dark leather sandals adorned his feet. His rich, dark brown hair complemented his well-kept beard. She wanted to study his facial features, but her view became blocked whenever the King turned in her direction. At the sight of his navy blue sash, a jolt shot through Daisy's body. Her mind raced through her memory bank, remembering the navy blue suit and shoes she had on at the time of her fall. She grabbed onto Roni's arm.

"Are you feeling all right?"

Daisy nodded, unsure of what just happened to her.

Picturing the navy blue suit and shoes triggered an inner awakening, causing her to do a double take. In silence she questioned, "Why am I here?"

Feeling unsure, she checked for the pink notebook and the yellow number-two pencil. Then she thought, "This venture into Niv has shaken me up. I have been prompted to look deep within my heart, which has caused me to change the value of some things that I once considered important. It has brought about a challenge to many choices I have made. So now, I am determined to hold on to these two things within my immediate possession—the notebook and the yellow number-two pencil. As small and insignificant as these items may seem to others, they are helping me to stay anchored in reality." With these thoughts she hugged the pink notebook and held firm to the yellow number-two pencil. She reasoned, "This Niv journey with Spotty has turned into a make-believe reality." Daisy made up her mind to pen these words, which she had just coined. She penned the words. Once she finished, her momentary unsteadiness concerning the navy blue sash passed.

Reverting her attention back onto the field, she watched as the King waved and greeted the crowd. The fans cheered him on as though he were the greatest champion of all. Caught up in the moment, she cheered too as the band played one exciting drum role victory march after another. Once the King and his entourage made their way to the exclusive seating area he waved once more and sat down. His entourage, everyone on the field, and all the spectators remained standing.

Daisy made another frustrating attempt to get a direct look at the King to study his features, but the flags and banners flying about the field blocked her line of sight.

Roni mentioned, "The band is beginning to play the province's national anthem, "We Surrender All."

Everyone stood and sang as they faced the direction of the King's box seat.

Noticing Daisy's confusion, Roni explained, "They are singing in the Province's native tongue, Hiroglif-ewigeleben."

In spite of her lack of understanding, the singing brought tears to Daisy's eyes. Once the singing ended, the team members stood before the King's viewing box and placed their nationality robes onto the ground, symbolizing their willingness to surrender. The audience applauded with appreciation and admiration.

The players rejoined their teams. Everyone remained standing and turned their attention to far most western sky. Daisy didn't have to ask, since she knew this signified the time for the fly-over, which normally follows the singing of the national anthem.

Daisy later penned these exact words within her journal relating to the fly-over:

After singing the national anthem, we all stood looking towards the western sky. Wearing the multi-dimensional sunglasses, I couldn't see anything at first. I began to wonder what we were looking for, but then what came into my line of sight took my breath away. A huge angelic figure with an ominous menacing face, topped with golden hair, protruding out of a metallic helmet, standing in a powerful chariot, pulled by a magnificent dominant white horse led a regiment of magnanimous, awe-inspiring, angelic figures, each driving a chariot.

Smoke billowed out and around from within the chariot's wheels. The lead driver's face moved back and forth peering over the crowd as if he searched the depth of our minds, our hearts and our souls. He appeared to be looking for something or someone who shouldn't be in the stands. I swallowed hard as I stood rigid next to Roni.

The fly-over that began as a mere speck off in the distance grew into an all-encompassing mass filling the entire sky over the grand colossal stadium. Like a huge storm front moving in, no one could have stopped or contained this force now hovering over the stadium.

I quaked in my penny loafers as not a sound came forth from the brigade of chariots; neither were any orders issued from the horsemen to the horses. Everyone stood in the stands and on the field speechless, breathless, and astounded. I didn't look to the right or to the left for fear that any movements might cause the great lead charioteer to glance my way. My knees shook so that I had to press the back of my legs against my seat for stability.

The leader banked his chariot towards the spectators, revealing glistening gold trim. The following ominous figures continued to move at a slow pace overhead. I closed my eyes for a brief moment, and I could hear a distant, slight roaring thunder.

His rugged fists clamped onto the reigns implied a power that could stop an entire army in its tracks. This lead figure's bare arms bore streamlined muscles with short black hairs. They revealed his veins that pulsated blood containing deep honor, pride, and justice. The horse's reigns fluttered, holding the force of space and time, and its mane ebbed and flowed with the air current.

The charioteer's evenly-toned, radiating, arm muscles scared me with their strength. His jeweled, dark purpled, velvet robe meshed with golden threads flowed and trailed with the wind, and even that commanded respect.

I thought, "How could an inanimate object command respect?" Again, I can only write in my limited vocabulary what I saw during this majestic fly-over.

The leader's sturdy breastplate shielded his heart. His eyes revealed him to be full of dignity, obedience, and sincere servitude. The paired groups of chariots following his lead and under his command had the same splendid adornment.

We remained standing and awestruck as they commandeered their chariots.

The power and force the charioteers displayed made my other previously viewed sporting event fly-overs seem like child's play. I had to chuckle because some of those fly-overs contained our powerful F/A-18A Hornets. I failed to conceive the nature of the mechanics of the prevailing machinery I observed at this flyover. The only thing I could register at that time had been my presence, and even that remained a mystery to me.

We continued to view the regimen following its leader. I could see a fearless determination within their eyes to stay in formation adhering to the lead chariot's unwavering command. These huge, powerful, all-encapsulating beings emitted a force of unlimited strength. They resonated with courage as their eyes shone clarity of purpose - void of animosity, regret, and doubt. They were pure unadulterated fortified magnificent beings demonstrating a power, a might, and an authority against which no one could stand.

As they overshadowed the entire stadium, I thought the massive arena's infrastructure would implode, taking me along with it. This lasted only for a brief moment and then we were looking at the back of the charioteers. Once again I swallowed hard as I took in the mere size and girth of the wheeled chariots, along with the powerful muscular horses and the mesmerizing billows of smoke.

I had never seen such honorable, commanding horses. Each horse had gracious adornment, along with fine grooming and tethering. Even the horse's bits shone with bright exquisiteness, which dispelled all weakness.

Once the charioteers cleared the stadium, they shot away at a breath-taking speed. In this explosive moment everyone fell backwards into the seats due to the shockwave. My hair flew up and back into my face as though someone had turned on an electric fan. The force even caused the multi-dimen-

sional glasses to be cast off my face. The noise still riveted deep within my ears. The g-force they exerted had made my outer epidermis layer stretch. Once everyone, including myself, got a grip on what had just happened, we couldn't be contained.

Over the intercom someone announced, "The King's regimen has broken the sound barrier, along with shattering the light barrier as well."

This added to the laugher, hollering, swooping and jumping occurring throughout the stadium. One would have thought that the teams had already played with a victory won. The mind-boggling emotional excitement of the fly-over event continued to fill the stadium.

A horn sounded and the King stood and gave his nod of approval over the great and mighty display of his provincial military capability.

Another round of excitement and frivolity carried on amongst the players, cheerleaders, and spectators for several more minutes.

Daisy's thoughts whirled as she questioned, "Who could ever stop this army, this force; who would even dare to try to stand up against them? Sheer power exuded from their countenance alone. We couldn't even utter a word in their presence, how then could someone even think to strike their hand against them?"

Roni said, "But that flyover consisted of just one tiny regiment of the King's vast army."

Upon this insight, Daisy had to take several deep slow breaths, willing herself not to hyperventilate. She had found the fly-over incomprehensible and now hearing Roni describe it as one tiny regiment blew her mind.

Daisy asked, "If this is the kind of effect just one fly-over can display, how powerful and mighty is this Provincial Army? And why am I even concerning myself with this matter?"

"Perhaps you are worried about something? Don't be afraid about the King's display of strength," Roni replied. "He enjoys showing his great army's power and might to proclaim that the victory has already been won. His armies are not bent on harming people, but have been designed to destroy the works of the Sly One. It is said, 'To the victor belongs the spoils.' Today we witnessed a portion of our victor's might."

"Thank you for explaining so many things for me. The fly-over had been more than I ever thought possible. It's just taking a while to sink in, that's all."

The band played another victory march as the spectators and the field cheered, affirming the King, proclaiming him the victor, and rejoicing in his grandeur.

After several minutes, the crowd settled down and the game of endurance commenced. Daisy found the game exciting and enjoyed being an active spectator. She recognized the American athletes straight away bearing the red, white, and blue patches on their jersey's sleeve. Every team player wore an emblem signifying their perspective country or land. Daisy found these items made the game even more interesting.

Daisy remained impressed how much the players ran throughout the entire game. The fans cheered, talked, and ate every kind of fresh fruit, nut, or delicacy provided from wandering vendors.

The children, Roni, and Daisy, were thrilled when it came time to stomp their feet for the kick points. She found this part of the game to be a great stress reliever. She'd think of things that troubled her and then she would visualize stomping them away.

Again, she tried to get a good look at the King's face. Every time she tried, something or someone blocked her view. Once she almost got to view his face straight on, but then he began to read the games pamphlet, shielding his face. Giving up, she decided she could study his features up close at the visitor's reception.

The game lasted about two and half hours. The Blue Diamonds Squared won the game and they were awarded a gold and titanium trophy. The taggers came in second.

"This has been an exciting game," proclaimed Daisy.

At the entry-level door on Sports Arena Way, Spotty whistled, "Over here Daisy."

Daisy said to Roni, "Spotty and I will come by your house after the visitor's reception."

Roni replied, "Okay. I am glad we got to enjoy the game together, and I can't wait until I see you again."

Daisy sensed that Roni's goodbye seemed more permanent than a simple see-you- later, good bye; especially as Candrise hugged Daisy, expressing a desire of not wanting to say goodbye.

Daisy squeezed the little girl tight and said, "We'll see each other later this evening." She turned to say good-bye to the boys, but they had run on ahead.

Roni called as she and Candrise waved and walked away, "I am glad we became friends. Au revoir, my friend."

Daisy's heart warmed knowing they had become friends and realizing she and Candrise had bonded. Still, Daisy thought Roni's departing words sounded more like a permanent goodbye. Shrugging it off, she and Spotty fell in step behind the crowd, making their way towards the palatial gardens.

Chapter Twenty Three:

EBB & FLOW

Utilizing the Glasgow coma scale again, Dr. Kabintzol ran another battery of tests.

He discussed the findings with the Zookers, "If my speculations are correct, these tests reveal that your daughter is on a gradual progression from the comatose state."

The doctor explained the graph scores of the tests, "According to the scale's results, sensations of pain have been registered at certain trigger points. Combine these findings with her varying hand and body movements would conclude a measurable improvement. Granted, your daughter isn't out of the comatose state yet, but she is making headway. The ongoing brain scans, blood tests, and stress tests also lead us to this conclusion."

Jonathan asked, "Doctor, you earlier indicated a moderate score somewhere between a range of twelve to thirteen. Could you please tell us the level of her coma now?"

"Daisy's chart now indicates a mild coma with a score ranging between thirteen and fourteen. These tests are based on a diagnosis of her respiratory patterns, pupillary responses, eye movements, and motor response. I would have to say, she is on the mend."

"Her family and I are more than happy with these findings, Doctor. We can't say thank you enough to you and your medical team for all you are doing for our daughter."

Martha held tight to his arm as Paul and Tulip stayed close to Daisy's bedside. The medical staff hovered near, checking the machines, reading over paperwork, and discussing the charts.

"It is quite possible," said the doctor, "for Daisy to regain consciousness any time now."

Tulip had invited Paul to be present during the morning's tests results. She saw the relief on his face as the doctor shared this good news.

Paul said, "I am so relieved."

"Paul, just think; it might be possible for us to speak with Daisy today."

Paul smiled and thought, "What will I say to her? And how will she respond? One thing's for sure; I will keep her safe in my arms. I love her, and this time I am going to win her heart."

A large group of people attended the team's visitors' reception. Daisy had been looking forward to touring the palace and for her chance to meet with the King. As they walked along, she and Spotty talked non-stop about his updated endangered species report.

"I am to present the report later today."

"Do you know exactly when?"

"Not yet. The King will call when it is time.

"I have made a few notes of my own," said Daisy, and she pointed to her notebook. "I thought I would come prepared to speak with the King."

"You are ever the true journalist, right Daisy?"

Daisy nodded.

The two made their way west on an avenue towards the palatial lawns. A large group of people swarmed the side palace gardens. Daisy overheard them talking about the endurance game. She watched everyone helping themselves to the delicious foods, party favors, and sparkling drinks provided on white linen-covered tables throughout the gardens and lawns.

"I find the gardens enchanting with all of the bountiful shrubs and flowing fountains. Spotty, I'd be lost in all these mazes of greenery if you weren't with me."

"Just don't go running off, I'm wanting to get inside the palace ahead of the crowd." But then he took some time to explain various foliages and inspiring figurines standing within the menagerie of flora along the paths.

Standing near the eastern side entranceway, Chris the American and Chu the Eskimo were engrossed in conversation. Still wearing their jerseys, the teammates turned to greet them. Daisy noticed Chris stood taller than Chu. He had an oval face with an olive complexion. Chu had jet-black hair with darker skin.

After introductions, Chu asked, "Did you enjoy the game today?"

"Yes, I did," said Daisy. "You made a remarkable goal kick at the end of the game."

Chris said, "Hey, what about me? I played a good game too."

Daisy laughed, "I watched you try to outrun the tagger who chased you. You almost made it to the goal box before him. All in all, you ran an exciting game. It was fun to watch."

Both the men laughed and carried on about game. Chris made a comment to Spotty, asking him about the view from atop the stands.

Daisy asked, "Chris, I noticed you wear an American emblem on your jersey. What state are you from?"

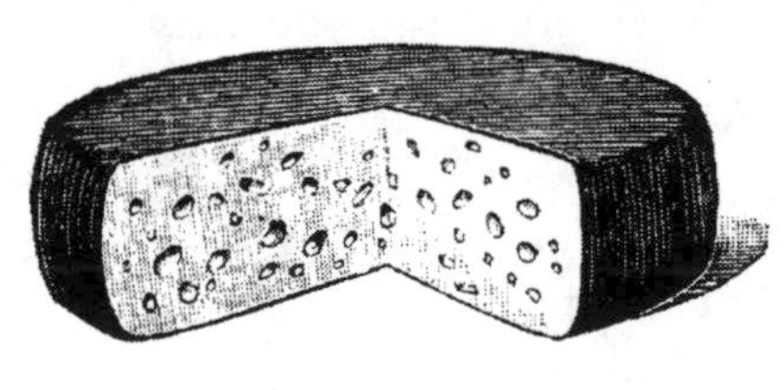

"I grew up in the cheese state of Wisconsin, and you?"

"I'm working in Indianapolis, and I rent an apartment downtown."

"I am quite familiar with that city."

A group of people headed over to converse with the two sportsmen. Spotty motioned to Daisy the time had come for them to be on their way. They thanked the two teammates for indulging them in conversation and said goodbye.

They made their way up a light-tan sandstone incline, which led into the side palace doors. This placed them onto the second level of the palace.

A young man held the door open and said, "Hi Spotty. Have you prepared an updated report for the King?"

"Hey there, Scheon. And yes, it's been six months since my last report. I'm ready as usual. By the way, I'd like you to meet Daisy."

"Hi Daisy, it's nice to meet you. I'm Scheon Mickealzs."

"It's nice to me you, Scheon," answered Daisy.

"Scheon, would you be so kind to accompany Daisy on a tour of the palace. I am expected in the endangered species wing."

"I'd be glad to provide Ms. Daisy a tour of the palace."

As he held out his arm for her, he told Spotty he would bring Ms. Daisy to his work area once they finished their tour.

Daisy looked at the professional, boyish teenager in his white shirt, bright blue tie and pressed black pants. While he showed her around the palace, he spoke well-using proper diction.

"Do you work full time at the palace?" Daisy asked.

"Yes. I enjoy my work as a palace guide. It reminds me of when I was a volunteer page at the House of Representatives."

"You seem a little young to be working for the government."

"Our school guidance counselor informed me about the

page program; and I filed an application on my sixteenth birthday. I and a couple other students were chosen to serve in the page program."

"What do pages do?"

"A page," explained Scheon, "helps within the offices and runs errands for members of the House of Representatives. I had an interest in political affairs and decided this opportunity would help me in my future career in government."

Daisy asked, "And how did you come to be here?"

"On one of my many page errands, I had been crossing a busy intersection within the capital city, and found myself in the province of Niv."

Biting her lower lip, Daisy looked at his peaceful, young face.

Scheon continued, "Upon my arrival into Niv, I assessed the place, met with the King, and discussed the many opportunities offered here. I decided to seek a job similar in nature. And now I work at the palace doing duties assigned on an as-need basis. Today, I had been informed to be ready to give Ms. Zookes a tour of the palace. I observed you and Spotty speaking with Chris and Chu in the side garden." Smiling, he added, "You see Ms. Daisy; it is my good pleasure to give you a tour, and to answer any and all questions you might have concerning the palace."

"I'm glad to have you as my very own tour guide." And she meant it, because she saw most people in small groups with a tour guide.

Scheon chuckled.

As they walked along Daisy commented, "The palace isn't anything like I had expected."

"And what did you expect?" asked Scheon.

"I had expected to see an abundance of all kinds of famous artwork, regal statues, glass-encased finery, golden artifacts, and splendid furniture throughout the building."

"The Palace is of a regal design and has stately furniture placed throughout," Scheon pointed out. "And, you will find some gold, silver, and crystal artifacts stationed every so often. But the King intended this building to be a working palace."

"This palace is the King's residence," Scheon continued. "He has his private living quarters on the third floor. The entire first and second floors are rooms and spacious wings set up for the general public to conduct meetings, facilitate projects, work on the provincial state of affairs, and perform ongoing operations of interest. We refer to it as the people's palace or the working palace."

As Scheon escorted Daisy, he said, "We will walk along the second-story inner sky walk. This walkway runs the full length of the palace straight through the center of the building. You will find this walkway permits one to view the activities on the first floor wings and enables us to gain entry into the second floor rooms along the sky walk. The rooms will be accessible on either side of the sky walk."

"I wondered why I didn't see any guards posted at the side

door when Spotty and I entered?"

"The palace," explained Scheon, "hasn't a need to post any guards at the doorways, but the front door does have a doorman or two provided as a courtesy for guests."

"Isn't the King concerned about vandals?"

"The palace doesn't need protected from thieves or vandals." He questioned, "Who in Niv would want to steal or break in, when we have free access to the palace? If you would like to take something, all you have to do is ask."

Daisy felt foolish for a moment, and then realized the young man had not been making fun of her. He had stated a simple fact: The province of Niv is vandalism-free.

"What a place," she said. "It must be nice to be free of thieves and vandals." Then she asked, "Do you ever have to lock things down or put in place a security system?"

"No, not within the province. I don't miss those hindrances."

Daisy said, "I wouldn't either. I think it's nice to be worry-free from ever having anything stolen. How grand to be permitted entrance into a magnificent building such as this without the presence of police or metal detectors. Come to think of it, I didn't even have to pay an admission fee."

Scheon nodded, understanding her comments.

"Scheon, I have no desire to take anything. I just want to look at what is on display. Thank you for informing me."

Scheon showed his boyish grin and said, "I appreciate your questions, and I'm glad you are taking the time to think things over."

Encountering groups along the passageway, Daisy took in the width of the sky walk, as they passed each other without interruption.

Instead of marble figurines and other pieces of art adorning the hallways, every so often Daisy and her escort happened upon a person or two, posing, standing on display.

Scheon explained, "These citizens also work at the palace. Their job is to be on display within the palace dressed in full garb representative of their culture and era. The King takes great pleasure in people. He isn't into purchasing items or relics for the palace. His relics are the people. He adorns his hallways and rooms with those who want to stand on display within the palace."

Daisy found it interesting to view such a variety of people on display.

"You will see an occasional piece of artwork, jewelry, or a golden object or two on display. But for the most part, it is the people who are his favorite works of art, his greatest treasures."

Daisy enjoyed encountering the various costumed people. She responded, "This place is fascinating. It appears as though every nation, land, and era is on display within the building or about the grounds."

"Visitors are permitted to speak with anyone on display."

"I think it would be less time consuming if I ask you about certain ones I want to know about. This approach will enable us to keep moving, as the palace is massive. Could you tell me about the couple dressed in full Indian garb?"

"The man is an Oneida Indian Chief standing with his wife," said Scheon. "They are arrayed in full Indian dress from the mid -1700's."

"Could you tell me about this next Elizabethan-looking soldier?"

"Oh yes, he is a Spanish soldier from the Renaissance and Elizabethan Age of Exploration who had been traveling to the New World."

"I think he looks magnificent in his full brimmed, brown hat with the rustic, colored feather," said Daisy. "Plus, his puffy shirtsleeves with the shorn matching skirt and tights make quite a fashionable statement. The leather gloves and the sword sheathed at his side all reflect a soldiery attire of the Romantic period. I'd say a time long past."

"Yes they do, and did you notice the gold chain and emblem hanging over his shiny silver breastplate? The emblem bore a symbol representing the queen of Spain."

Walking on, Daisy asked about a solitary woman standing on display.

"She is Deborah the prophetess and judge from old – between 1209 and 1169 BC. She is an honored leader."

"I'm glad to learn ancient-day women had positions of leadership, in spite of the prevailing dominating male attitude."

Inspired by this female leader, Daisy scanned her unassuming robe with its belt tied about her waist. Her long reddish-brown hair hung over her outer cloak. The way the cloak laid about her shoulders gave her an air of authority and wisdom, and her eyes showed great discernment. Daisy thought, "She belongs in this great hall along with the other amazing figures standing on display adorning the palace."

"I would like to ask you about so many of the people, but I am anxious to keep moving and to see the rest of the Palace."

Scheon replied, "We'll keep moving, it's alright."

Daisy thought, "Maybe I'll come back with Roni later. My main mission today is to meet with the King. Spotty is to meet with him later and I have some questions of my own to ask him."

Scheon saw the anxiousness in her eyes; "As soon as we are done touring I will take you to Spotty. I'm sure your meeting with the King will be pleasant."

Scheon drew her focus back to the displays saying, "The people considered it a privilege and an honor to stand on display within the palace. A schedule has been established and a rotating shift of provincial citizens participate in the display program."

Daisy listened as Scheon instructed her about the work taking place in the Palace. He shared, "Business meetings are being conducted and other groups studying work projects hold sessions within the conference rooms."

They ventured into a room filled with a group of architects. The group had been poring over draft sketches of a city under construction. Scheon pointed to the craftsman books, writing instruments, drafting tools, and all kinds of blueprints and layouts filling the room. The group paid no attention to Scheon and Daisy in the doorway, as they conferred over a cedar desk discussing weights, measurements, and materials, along with stresses of torque and compound structural notations.

Daisy asked, "What does the picture on the back wall signify? It's the picture of a single cut, square stone with the inscription, The Chief Corner Stone, - The stone that the builders rejected."

Scheon answered, "It is a reminder to the architects and builders to never allow this to happen again."

"Why? I don't understand. Did this happen before?"

"Yes it did, and as we continue the tour I think you will come to understand."

As he led Daisy down the sky walk he continued, "The architects are busy designing and laying out the new city. It's under construction behind this great city of Niv. We can get a glimpse of it through the far north end of the palace. I'll show it to you once we reach that portion of the sky walk."

"Wow, a new city. I think this one is spectacular; I can't imagine a reason to build and design another."

Coming to the center atrium of the palace, Scheon and Daisy viewed the palace's grand entrance hall. The spacious entrance hall had a white marble tiled floor accentuated with swirls of mauve and gray. Looking over the right sky walk's railing, Scheon pointed to a large compass. The compass had been impregnated into the floor. Multi-colored inlaid slate tile formed the design of the large colored compass. It contained varying shades of blues, rusts, grays, and peaches.

"The interesting shades of slate and its texture makes the compass's design pop. This use of shading lends it a multi-dimensional appearance," said Daisy.

"The compass's main arm points true north. The builder set the compass in place to show the way to the King's council. Directly beyond the grand entrance hall lies the King's lecture hall. It can be entered from the first or second level." He pointed to a short passageway leading to double doors. "The doors are closed; this signifies the King and the council are in session."

"Is this where Spotty will present his report?"

"Yes it is."

From here on, the tour took on a more serious nature.

They passed another set of conference rooms filled with dignitaries combing the governing documents for the province of Niv. Scheon would only stand in the doorway with Daisy at his side. These governing rooms had an air of high importance and it became obvious to Daisy they were discussing serious matters.

Continuing along the sky walk towards the southern front of the King's palace she could view an adjoining set of rooms called the Ebb and Flow Sanctuary. Scheon directed Daisy to the left of the sky walk to view this area. She watched as several babies were being attended to under the watchful care of loving women. In an adjoining area she could see children of all ages under adult supervision.

"Is this the city's nursery or day care facility?" asked Daisy. "And to whom do these infants and children belong?" She found it sweet to hear the children's voices and the cooing of the infants.

"On the far border of the province lies the Naive Sea. Every morning as the tide ebbs and flows, it washes these little ones onto the shores of Niv. These are the un-named, the weak, and the small ones in search of love

and affection. The city receives them with open arms. They are gathered and brought into the palace to be doted on and cared for by the palace's parental staff." Daisy saw the cheerful staff members providing a service for each little one. Scheon continued, "They are each given a name or a new name, whichever the case, and their names are written in the book."

"Oh, it is such an endearing sight. Did you say they are washed ashore? How is it possible?" Then Daisy said, "Don't answer, for I am wondering how I came to be here. Just tell me more about the children."

Scheon explained further, "Throughout the day, various citizens come and claim each and every child. I am sure you noticed people loafing about the market place, hanging around socializing."

"Yes, I did," said Daisy. "I remember seeing many people milling about on my outing with my friend Roni."

"Those citizens come from the outer region of the province. They travel daily into the city and take the little ones home with them. It happens everyday. A new batch of infants and children wash onto the shores, and a new batch of citizens take the babes and children home, just like the tide. That is why this room is named the Ebb and Flow Sanctuary."

Daisy had been touched at the open display of compassion and love for these small helpless ones. She watched as one adult after another entered into the inner rooms and chose a child.

Scheon interjected, "Everyday all of them are claimed; none are left behind."

A sobering scene to witness, Daisy thought. "How unconscionable for so many little ones to be abandoned into the Sea of Naivety, left to fend for themselves in the end." It took her a few minutes to get her wits about her.

Scheon gave her some time to absorb the insurmountable passion of this ongoing, working palace. They continued down the sky walk turning right at the far northwest end of the building. He said, "Spotty works in this end of the palace. This is the area where he meets and facilitates with his team members, called the endangered species management team."

Daisy stood on the sky walk looking over his area full of tables covered with literature and bookshelves lining the walls. A spiral staircase descended into the area where Spotty worked.

Scheon said, "By the way, we can view the new city under construction through this area."

Daisy had been studying the room, watching Spotty work with another person. She answered, "Thanks Scheon. I would like to see the new city. I still can't get the Ebb and Flow Room out of my mind. Of all the areas you showed me, those rooms moved me the most. I suppose this doesn't surprise you?"

"The Ebb and Flow Sanctuary always seems to have a profound effect on all the visitors."

Daisy said, "I did enjoy your tour. Thanks for showing

me around and for all of the detailed explanations. "

Spotty looked up from his work and saw Scheon and Daisy conversing on the sky walk. He yelled, "Hey you two, come on down here and visit for a while."

A spiral staircase wound its way to this first level room. Spotty greeted them as he thanked Scheon for giving Daisy a tour. Scheon gave a quick overview about the different areas and wings he showed Daisy throughout the building as Daisy interspersed approving words of delight over the tour.

Spotty ushered them around his working area and began to show Daisy his team's office. He described the various rooms for conducting business and holding conferences.

Then he led her and Scheon through a door leading outside to the back palatial lawns. It caught Daisy off guard to see animals wandering about the grounds. The animals were kept separated from the front palatial grounds. The lawns area ran deep into a wooded area for miles, with plenty of trees and open expanses for roaming.

"This is where many extinct or near-extinct plants and animals species live during the transition to the new city. The animals roam as far as they want, but tend to keep a respectful distance not to disturb the workers and builders constructing the new city."

Scheon pointed, saying, "The new city is being developed across the far end of the property."

Daisy looked off on her right and could just glimpse the

shining new city under construction on a distant hillside. "It shines even brighter than the city of Niv."

Then she heard and saw a herd of Okapi running in the area. They distracted her from the city being built. She watched as the Okapi stuck out their long tongues to eat berries from a tree. She and Scheon started laughing, amused by the length of the animals' tongues.

Spotty said, "I don't find anything funny about the animals eating."

"Oh come on, Spotty, you have to admit. They do have unusually long tongues."

Spotty rolled his eyes.

Once the three finished sightseeing outside, they re-entered the Endangered Species Management Center.

Scheon put on his tour guide manner again and talked about the office design. As with all the rooms within the palace, the walls were of a regal color and texture. The high ceilings with windows permitted a generous amount of natural light to pour in, illuminating the entire area. The desks and bookshelves were constructed of rich mahogany and cedar woods. The marble floor consisted of maroon and white hues, and column structures exposed the sky walk from where he and Daisy had toured the palace.

Spotty had been dictating his report to another gentleman at one of the desks when the two arrived. At Spotty's insistence, he asked Daisy to preview his report.

Daisy recognized much of the information contained within the report from what he had shared with her as they conversed along Begin Again Thoroughfare. Daisy found Spotty's team to be very enthusiastic about their work. She listened as they told stories about their safari excursions, mentioned their prior dealings at zoology parks, and shared a brief encounter on an aquatic mission. For them, fulfillment meant a life amongst the animal kingdom.

Daisy inferred, "I have come to a conclusion about this place. Everyone who lives here can find a hobby or job of interest to connect and become involved within the province of Niv. All the citizens desire to belong and become a part of vision and purpose set in motion here." Sharing this realization cemented her appreciation of and fondness for the place and the people all the more. Spotty, Scheon, and the other workers nodded with approval.

To Daisy's surprise, Spotty announced, "Break time." His colleagues served a meal. The splendid meal consisted of multi-grain muffins, creamy soups, fresh vegetables, toasted nuts with honey, and ended with sweet milk. As they ate, the group conversed about wildlife concerns.

After the meal, Daisy stood to stretch. Hoping to meet with the King soon, she needed to move around since her patience was beginning to wane. As she stretched her legs, she turned in the direction of the spiral staircase. She spied a door angled behind the staircase. The door had been to her back when she entered the endangered species management center. Stepping closer, she read a sign posted on the door. The sign read: The King's Most Cherished and Precious Endangered Species Concern. With a puzzled expression, Daisy looked over her shoulder at Spotty.

Albeit too late, Spotty yelled, "Wait!"

Daisy had turned the handle and entered the room, with the door closing behind her. She waited for her eyes to adjust due to the dim lighting in the room. Walking to the center of the small room, she scanned the four walls. Floor to ceiling mirrors covered the entire expanse of the four walls within the empty room. Daisy stood staring at her reflection, restating the words posted on the door. "The King's Most Cherished and Precious Endangered Species Concern."

After repeating the words, a lightning bolt shot through her senses as she realized the enormity of their meaning. She remained staring at her lone reflection for what seemed like an eternity. Absorbing the impact she said to herself, "How can this be? No, oh no, this can't be right. I'm not on any endangered species list. Someone's got this all wrong." She took deep breaths, trying to remain calm. She crossed her arms and began rubbing them, as if to fend off a chill. This brought her some comfort as she tried to accept the impact of knowing she had been listed on the endangered species list. Again, she spoke aloud, "I didn't see my name on Spotty's report. He could have said something." She shut her eyes tight and then opened them slowly, wishing away her image in the mirrors.

Daisy had never thought about human existence in these finite terms. Now she wondered, "Would man's existence come to an end, even after all the research, discoveries, cures, and inventions? Do we simply die off or fade away?" She further questioned, "Has life been predetermined, making it impossible to stop the hands of time bent on man's destruction." She felt saddened, knowing life as she knew it would end.

Her sadness turned to fear as she thought of the unknown, "What's going to happen to me? Is this place called Niv my final destiny? Am I to facc this life ending news alone, apart from my family and friends? This is way too much to comprehend."

She began to feel anxious. This concept disturbed her heart, mind, and soul. She yelled at her image, "I don't want to die. I want to live. I want my mother and father, and my sister and friends to live. Isn't there any hope for our future?" Finding the room too much to bear, she turned to leave. She hesitated. Seeing her image on another wall, she held back her tears. She felt like lashing out at something, anybody, but whom? Alone in the room with her stark cold reflection, she became aware of the truth staring back at her. Daisy refrained from crying and exited the room.

Those waiting on the othcr side uf the door understood

the gravity of her encounter in the mirrored room. Spotty and Scheon consoled her as best they could.

After a moment of reprieve she said, "Spotty, I thought it had been the plants and animals you and the King were so concerned about. After all, I did look over your updated endangered species report, and I didn't read anything about my demise. Maybe in your haste, you somehow failed to mention man in your endangered report. Would you care to enlighten me about this fact?"

Spotty could feel her anger and said, "Daisy it is my job to provide an updated endangered species report to the King. And, I— along with the King and others—am aware of man's predicament of becoming extinct. But putting it into words just didn't seem right. I believed you had enough to contend with on your journey along the thoroughfare."

Daisy replied, "But we had several detailed discussions about this topic." Angered even more she asked, "Why leave out the part about me, about man? You must have known this since it is your work and your passion."

Spotty said, "And that's why I led you here."

Daisy exclaimed, "What?"

Everyone in the room remained silent, seeing the anguish in the woman's face. Spotty and Scheon continued to console Daisy about this all-important matter.

Scheon interjected, "Daisy there is a time for telling and a time to remain silent. Perhaps now you are ready to hear the story."

"Go on Scheon," said Daisy, "I'm listening."

Scheon proceeded to tell Daisy a story, "Daisy, metaphorically speaking it happened this way. Man became lazy and callous, forgetting to tether his sail to the mast of the boat. It began with these two people, a bright young couple. They

were in a boat sailing the sea following a charted course. They could see the wondrous lighthouse off in the distance. They were following it to the Shores of Promise. But as they sailed along they became lazy, caught up in their own fun and games, and their hearts became callous. The trip through the sea lasted longer than they had hoped. In their slothfulness, they forget to tether their sails to the mast of the boat. Then one day, the deep raised its head and swallowed them up."

Daisy asked Scheon to stop a moment as she took out her pink notebook and the yellow number-two pencil. She thought this story would be of some significance and she wanted to write it down.

Scheon continued, "A tempest blew the couple off course. Their boat plunged in many directions. They lost sight of the lighthouse. Now frightened, they tried to find their own way through the sea to the Shores of Promise. They fought against the tempest, but without the sail being tethered it became a senseless, useless, unmatchable fight. Once the deep swallowed up their boat, they swam and fought their way through the sea. The deep proved to be a ruthless and relentless taskmaster.

Many years later, the King came sailing along in a fine, handsome ship. The King and his father had built the ship. His father sent him on a mission to search for those whom the deep held captive and for those still swimming in the sea trying to make a futile way to the Shores of Promise. He would sail to the distant Shores of Promise with the wondrous lighthouse in view. An avid sailor, the King remained astute and safety conscious, He double-checked his tethered sail. His father had procured an anchor to hold the ship fast.

The ferocious tempest blew the King's ship fighting against him. Seeing the King had not been slack in his rigging or lacking in his devotion to stay afloat, the tempest became devious. The tempest cheated in its fight against the King and incited the creatures of the deep to rise up against the King on his mission. When this didn't work, the tempest became infuriated in its fight against the unsinkable boat of the King. As a last resort, the tempest utilized a mischievous plan to capsize the King's boat.

"The tempest deceived those

swimming in the sea about the King. Lying, he led them to believe the King's ship and mission would lead them even further away from the distant Shores of Promise. Then, a large group of swimmers congregated around the King's ship and pushed it onto its side, capsizing the boat.

"The rope attached to his father's anchor wrapped around the King's foot and plunged the King down into the depths of the great deep.

"A small band of swimmers, who didn't believe the tempest, thought all had been lost when they came upon the King's overturned ship, realizing he had plummeted to the bottom of the deep. But the sea that covered the deep and the wind of the tempest discussed what had happened. The sea and the wind knew of the King's father and were subject to obey the laws of the land. They watched how the tempest cheated and tricked the people into capsizing the King's ship, which resulted in the King's apparent demise, deterring him from his mission.

The sea and the wind investigated the ship's tethered sail and saw the cut rope of the anchor, making the sinking of the King's ship contrary to the laws set in place. Using discernment, they reasoned this unforeseeable disaster should not have occurred and the deep had no right to hold the King captive or lay claim to his ship.

"After a couple of days plus one, the deep shook with a violent quaking and the bottom of the sea split wide open. The sea and the wind rejoiced at this quaking and worked on the King's behalf. The wind blew and the sea churned, enabling the King and several others whom he had rescued to be released from the prison of the deep. Those whom the King rescued had come to believe in the King's mission. They were willing to put their trust in his unsinkable ship and journey with him to the distant shore.

The sea recovered the King's capsized ship and with the help of the wind the ship flipped over and floated upright once again. The wind filled the sails and the sea pushed it in the direction of the King and all the people with him in the water. They had drifted a great distance from the Shores of Promise where the wondrous lighthouse stood, but the King knew his way through these uncharted waters. As the mighty ship sailed along, they picked up others whom they found treading the waters, desiring to be named among them.

So you see, Daisy, it's not the King who fails to tether his sail. We fail to tether the sail. The King comes in search of us, despite our laziness, despite our foolishness, and despite our unwillingness to stay tethered. He came to chart our course to reach the distant shore guided by the lighthouse stationed on the Land of Promise. His ship is the only way we can get there. Many are treading the waters of the sea, but the deep always wants to swallow them up and hold them captive. Devious creatures lurk in the sea, which we must flee from and avoid, at all cost. The King's ship is the one sure way to reach the distant shore. And on this journey, one has to keep the lighthouse in view to stay on course.

If we remain in the sea, the deep will never give up its hold. The tempest still blows and oftentimes it is unrelenting. But now, it hasn't any power over the King's vessel.

"For the rules set in motion long ago state that a ship can only be sunk one time, and only once. Since the King's ship has already been there and back, the deep has no power or hold on him. His recovered vessel holds a great hoard of survivors, and remains forever unsinkable."

Daisy stopped writing and the room grew silent.

Scheon said, "So Daisy I ask you, are your sails tethered to the mast? Is the anchor in your life weighing you down or holding you fast? We make an attempt to build, to succeed, and to go where we want in our own strength. But the journey is too difficult and the tempest too big and unruly. The King has a seat for you on his vessel. We can ride and sail with him, because according to the endangered species report man cannot make it on his own. We are all in danger of becoming extinct; we are all endangered, finite species. With the King's provision we can reach a harbor of safety and enjoy his island of peace where the lighthouse stands shining with hope on the faithful Shores of Promise, breathing in his love."

Daisy looked at Spotty, and then at Scheon. She became aware of the others in the room now focusing their attention onto her. She got up from the table, leaving her notebook and the yellow number-two pencil.

She said, "I want to meet with the King; I want to meet with him now."

Spotty heard the agitation in her voice and said, "We have to wait until it is our turn. I don't think we should interrupt his meetings."

Overcome with a sense of urgency and motivated to act, Daisy stated, "I want to see him now."

With those words Daisy made a quick exit up the spiral staircase and ran back down the sky walk toward the closed set of doors she and Scheon had passed earlier. Placing her hand on the L-shaped knob of the solid cherry doors, she barged in.

The King sat at the head of an assembly conducting a formal business meeting. He looked up from the table of discussion and locked eyes with Daisy. Instantly, she couldn't move. She couldn't speak. Locked in his gaze, she became stuck in time.

The expectant group at the hospital waited to witness Daisy spring forth from her coma. They became devastated when her heart monitor's alarm sounded and the screen signified heart failure. Still convening in the room, the doctor and medical staff kicked into full STAT mode. A nurse escorted the family into the hall as the medical team performed Cardiopulmonary Resuscitation (CPR).

Dr. Kabintzol shined his flashlight into her pupils while

a staff member performed CPR; another staff member cautioned about her bruised ribs. They were intent on resuscitating the patient. The trained trauma team performed this routine movement as their training kicked into high gear with a life at the precipice of no return.

Jonathan, Martha, Tulip, and Paul congregated in the hallway outside of Daisy's doorway. They wept and held onto each other through this startling change of events.

Locked in the King's gaze, all the elements of the peripheral world around Daisy melted into a shade of oblivion. The only thing she could see had been his eyes and the light shining from them. As his eyes bore into hers, she couldn't even

remember the reason why she had come barging into the room. The King spoke first and said with his eyes, "Tell me, what do you want?"

As she looked into his all-encompassing eyes, Daisy searched her memory bank for something, anything, but words failed. Those pure eyes commanded authority, understood all knowledge, exuded understanding, and radiated life. Piercing her heart and delving into her soul, his stare held her between space and time. She felt insignificant to ask anything from him, the King.

Again the King spoke with his eyes and this time he added her name, "Tell me Daisy, what is it you want?" Like a small balloon being deflated, Daisy asked a question, "Why did Spotty bring me here?"

The King knew she had become upset with Spotty and said, "Think again Daisy, what brought you here to the province of Niv?"

Continuing the CPR, the doctor ordered the defibrillator be brought and used. When her parents saw the machine enter into the room, they held their breaths and clung to each other. The trauma team attached all the cords and powered the defibrillator machine and shot a jolt of electric current through Daisy's struggling comatose body.

Daisy could not blink her eyes, as they remained locked onto the King's. But when the King blinked, she spiraled down into a milky chasm into the depths of another dimension. Void of mass or material, she careened through open space and stopped. A part of the past week of her life flashed before her like a movie screen. She saw herself back at the Benson Building entering the east stairwell wearing her navy blue suit.

When the spiraling stopped she answered the King whose eyes had stopped her spiral, "Spotty didn't bring me to the province. The fall brought me here to this place." At once her anger towards Spotty subsided.

The King smiled as his eyes remained transfixed holding her firm and he questioned her, "What are you afraid of Daisy?" Then he blinked again.

The trauma team yelled, "Clear," shooting another volt of current through her semi-responsive body. Her heart would beat arrhythmically at times and then it would flat line. This baffled the staff. The doctor thought she must have developed a blot clot, which could account for her current distress.

Once again, Daisy spiraled down entering another dimension outside of the province of Niv or any other world she knew. The King's gaze held her and she stopped in mid-landing. Having seen other segments of her life flash before her, she answered the King, "I am afraid of dying." This had been more of a confession than an answer.

The King's eyes replied, "Fear is a terrible master. What else are you afraid of Daisy?" The King blinked once more.

Again the trauma team yelled, "Clear," and shot one more volt of electric current through Daisy's body.

In the hallway, her family overheard the trauma team's attempts to save her. They became more distraught with each passing second.

Daisy spiraled down again and held onto his locked eyes. She feared if she even attempted to let go or blink, she might freefall forever. She blurted out much more loudly this time, "I am afraid of living too. Keeping busy helps me to avoid dealing with certain issues, especially my fears. The busier I keep myself, the more excuses I can make for why I do or say some things. I guess it's a coping mechanism."

The King's all-knowing eyes nodded, affirming this fear that held her captive. This time he did not blink. He asked her, "And now, what do you want?"

After unsuccessful attempts with CPR and the defibrillator machine, the doctor ordered an injection of beta blockers. Their concerns about losing Daisy heightened. The team hoped the beta blockers injection would produce the response needed and bring a registering heartbeat on the heart monitor.

Calmed now, the King's eyes seemed to have melted her insecurity, which had driven her to run in a tiff to him in the first place.

"I want to be free," said Daisy. "I don't want to be afraid anymore."

After she finished her simple statement and request, the King nodded.

Just then, the locked transmission between them ceased and Daisy free fell through a wide-open funnel in a creamy fog. Her hair blew straight up and her VEESA badge flew up

over her head and away. As she sank down into the tunnel she yelled. It reminded her of younger days when she rode a thrill ride at an amusement part.

The nurse brought the syringe of beta blockers into the room and gave it to the doctor. He had been checking Daisy with his stethoscope when the first gentle, even heartbeat registered across the monitor. Whatever ride his patient had been on had come to an end. He and the team were grateful because now her vital signs were normal. The heart monitor registered a regular heartbeat, her breathing stabilized, and all was well with the patient aside from the coma. They found it unnecessary to use the beta blockers injection.

Jonathan and Martha approached the doctor and asked what had caused this sudden heart problem with their daughter.

The doctor said, "We are relieved as you are she came through this traumatic moment. What caused her heart to enter into duress, I do not know. We will continue to monitor her vital signs. I wish I could tell you more. Right now, she is stable and resting."

Tulip held onto Paul's arm as they approached Daisy's bedside. All four were overcome with anxiety at the prospect of almost having lost her. It had been a long week.

Daisy found herself strolling a beach swinging her arms. Her shoes dangled from her left hand. Her khaki pants were rolled up halfway to her knees with her bare feet sloshing the water on the distant shore. Her legs willed her forward as the wind blew her hair.

She came upon a turtle waddling up the sandy slope of the beach in search of a place to lay her eggs. She guessed it to be a marine turtle. She smiled thinking Spotty would have gone into a dissertation about its habitat and endangered status. As the tide continued to ebb and flow, she became aware of where she was. Up ahead, she saw the beacon of the lighthouse. With an all-encompassing peace invading her soul, she exclaimed, "It's the Shores of Promise. I'm going home."

Chapter Twenty Four:

FAMILY REUNION

All had been quiet, and the day had turned to evening. In the stillness she turned her head and saw Paul sitting next to her hospital bed keeping vigil. His eyes moistened as he gave her a warm endearing smile. The long five-day wait had come to an end.

"Oh, Paul," mouthed Daisy as her eyes filled to the brim, overcome with joy at seeing him, keep watch over her.

Paul took hold of her hand, kissing it while speaking words of endearment. Their souls had found their mates. He loved her and she wanted to be loved by him.

Now, no longer afraid to receive his love, Daisy's fear of entering into a committed relationship with this fine, handsome man dissipated. They locked hands and stared into one another's eyes. Words seemed out of place for this bonding moment. Daisy had been brought back to life and Paul thanked the prince of peace.

Returning from having pie and coffee at the hospital's cafeteria, Daisy's parents and Tulip entered the room. They hurried to her bedside crying tears of joy and relief.

"Hi Sis," greeted Tulip. Daisy thought back to when she had last heard her sister's voice. It had been at the cascading falls near the entrance of the city of Niv.

Daisy made an earnest attempt to tell this to Tulip, but her vocal cords couldn't produce any sound, plus she had a severe case of cottonmouth. An incoherent jumble of thoughts ran through her mind, causing her to feel bewildered.

Tulip patted her sister's shoulder and said, "Just rest Daisy. Tomorrow and the days ahead, we will have all the time to catch up on things." Tulip buzzed for the nurse.

Paul offered Martha his bedside chair. Daisy thought her mother looked much smaller and frailer than she had before. She grasped her mother's hand and mouthed the word, "Mother."

The way she tried to say the word strengthened Martha's weakened posture. She wept, holding on to her daughter.

Not wanting to be left out, Jonathan cleared his throat. Daisy looked at her loving father and whispered, "Daddy." This rhetorical reversion to childhood made his heart soar. He puffed up his chest giving the appearance of the strong father figure his feeble daughter needed. Being reunited with his daughter meant the world to Jonathan J. Zookers; his two girls were his pride and joy.

In the meantime, Paul had left the room affording the Zookers privacy with their daughter. He telephoned Darla's cell phone with the good news.

Working at Michelangelo's Ice Cream Parlor, Darla shared the news with several patrons and friends. Phoning Ted Strain's emergency number, she dialed him to let him know Daisy had emerged from the coma.

The evening staff shared in the family's joy at seeing Ms. Zookes coherent and trying to communicate. The head nurse paged her doctor who had gone home for the evening. Exhausted from a full day of testing and procedures, Dr. Kabintzol asked the overseeing evening physician to check in on Ms. Zookes; and he asked to speak with Daisy's father.

Dr. Kabintzol said, "Good evening Jonathan. The nurse just informed me your daughter is awake and responsive."

"That's right Doctor. It's amazing. We are trying to keep our excitement down, since she appears very weak."

"That's very wise of you Jonathan. I wouldn't expect too much at the beginning, you know. Most patients coming out of a coma need a few days to adjust. I also wanted to let you know, I have asked the nurse to contact the evening physician. His name is Dr. Dutch Boyland; he will see to Daisy's care tonight. It's been a long day."

"I understand Doctor. You need to spend some time with your family as well. Please do. We feel she is in good care, and I am sure Dr. Boyland will do a fine job looking over our Daisy. Thank you for speaking with me."

"You're welcome, and I'll see you tomorrow. Goodnight

Jonathan. Be sure to tell your wife how glad I am for the news."

"I will. Goodnight Doctor." Jonathan trusted the doctor's judgment to utilize the evening physician, and knew better than anyone that the doctor needed a rest and some time with his own family as well.

Dr. Dutch Boyland reported to Daisy's room after being paged and having a brief telephone conversation with Dr. Kabintzol. He had been somewhat familiar with Daisy's case.

The doctor approached Daisy's bedside and began asking her routine questions, while her family hovered in the background.

He began, "Welcome back Ms. Zookes from your week-long sleep."

Daisy half nodded feeling woozy, yet she did recognize the all-familiar smells of anesthetics, hospital odors, and emergency equipment.

The doctor asked, "Ms. Zookes, do you know where you are?"

Daisy's mouthed the words, "The hospital."

The doctor said, "That's correct. My name is Dr. Boyland." Then he asked, "Do you recognize these people standing behind me?"

Daisy gave him an affirmative nod.

This pleased the doctor, showing some of her memory intact.

He asked, "Do you remember falling in the stairwell at

work?"

Daisy shook her head no, then thought a moment and changed her response to a yes.

The doctor said, "You did indeed fall - on Tuesday morning. It is now Saturday evening."

Daisy drifted off as he shared this information with her. He continued with a short physical examination. The doctor advised the family to take it slow with Daisy and to keep any questions basic and simple.

He said, "Her mental and emotional state appeared to be normal, but it's wise to take small steps in the beginning."

The family agreed and fought off the urge to become overly emotional in her presence.

It didn't take long before Daisy fell sound asleep, as she was very weak. This concerned the family, but the nurse staved off their worries, reassuring the family the patient had indeed fallen asleep.

Paul kept the evening vigil at Daisy's bedside, while Tulip and her parents went to their hotel for a much-needed sleep after nights of tossing, turning, and worrying.

Daisy awoke at 4:00 a.m. in the quiet hospital noticing a few attendants passing outside in the hall. She proceeded to itch the end of her nose with the splint holding her right hand middle finger and ring finger. Next she lifted her swollen left hand to view the Intravenous medical line (IV) attached streaming fluids into her body. She wondered what types of medicines were carousing through her veins. She ran her fingers over the butterfly stitches on the top of her forehead, discovering a large cut.

She made an effort to sit up because she wanted to get out of bed. Paul had fallen asleep in the lounge chair and she didn't wish to wake him. After feeling her cut forehead, she became curious to see what other cuts and bruises she had sustained as a result of the fall.

As she squirmed in the bed, Nurse Mary Billie came into the room on a scheduled round to check on her. Not wanting to wake Paul either, she smiled at Daisy and spoke in hushed tones.

The nurse asked, "How are you feeling."

Daisy mouthed, "Okay." Then she motioned if she could get out of bed.

Then nurse instructed, "It is better for you to wait until morning once you've had a visit from your doctor. Besides, your left leg might not hold you up since you twisted it in multiple places."

Daisy had been unaware of this injury. The nurse gave Daisy a rub-down and a back massage, which helped her to relax. Giving her some ice water, the nurse left the room. Overcome with exhaustion, she realized it would be a while before she regained her strength. The rub-down did her good, along with the nurse's company.

Daisy relaxed and began to reminisce about the province

of Niv. Now, she questioned if it had all been a dream or if she had visited such a place. She probed her mind questioning how would she ever know. She decided not to speak to anyone about her experience in Niv. She figured if she spoke the dream aloud, this could somehow make Niv be only a fantasy. Daisy wanted to hold onto her adventure into the province and didn't want it to float away and disappear like a mirage. Plus, she'd give anything to have that pink notebook with all of her notes. It had been an interesting time spent in the province-—real or not -—and she had learned plenty.

"Huh," she said to herself, "Maybe that's why I feel so tired." She repositioned her pillow, took one more glance at Paul sleeping, and then closed her eyes.

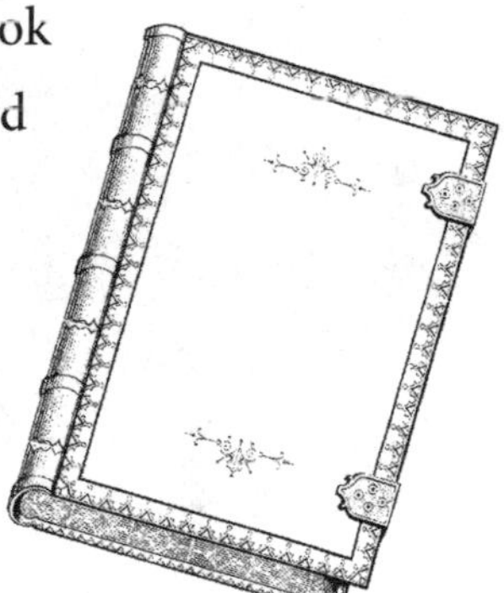

Chapter Twenty Five:

THE NOTEBOOK

Dr. Kabintzol came to see Daisy early in the morning. He did a routine check of her vitals and asked her questions to test her reasoning skills. The doctor found her to be in good mental health. He suggested she be moved to the on-going care and rehabilitation wing of the hospital.

She would receive extended care for regaining muscle strength. Plus, keeping Daisy in close proximity provided extra time to oversee her recovery. With each passing day, Daisy's breathing became steadier and the occasional head pains subsided. The medical team kept the intravenous drip attached to her arm pushing fluids and medications to ward off infection.

Her parents and Tulip came to see her everyday, and Paul stayed at her side. Darla stopped in often.

Daisy worked hard during the physical rehabilitation workouts. She became exhausted in the afternoons and would take long naps. Having Paul as her confidant provided an added incentive.

She continued the healing process under the guided care of the trauma center team. The physical therapy she received proved positive. They tested and retested her speech, sight, hearing, and smell, along with her cognitive skills to eliminate any brain malfunctions.

Her sizable skull fracture was on the mend, but the doctor advised her not to take up jogging or running anytime soon. Also, the doctor set up a one-year schedule for follow-up visits, every three months. She walked with crutches as her leg healed. Her bruised right collarbone remained stiff. Due to her cracked ribs, she did breathing treatments to keep her lungs clear. The deep gash on her forehead would leave only a faint scar once the stitches dissolved. The broken fingers on her right hand set with a metal splint inhibited her ability to write. Along with being bruised, the doctor noted a hairline crack in her left arm and kept it wrapped for stability. This remained sore to movement.

After her third day in the rehabilitation wing, Ted Strain accompanied Darla on a visit to the hospital.

Strain asked, "How are you feeling, Ms. Zookes?"

"I am doing much better. Thank you for asking. How are things at work?"

"We are as busy as ever," interjected Darla, "Everybody has been asking about you."

"Are you up to discussing work and the progress of the adventure story for Davenport?" asked Strain.

"Yes, I am feeling well enough to concentrate on work. I hope to get out of the hospital as soon as I can."

"Oh. Do you think it is wise to rush things?"

"I don't feel rushed," said Daisy. "Besides, the doctor said I am progressing and he feels I could go home as early as next week."

Darla said, "That's great Daisy."

"Well," continued Strain, "I wanted to talk to you about work. I had asked Ms. Firkens to cover for you while your were incapacitated. She has been busy researching information and developing a story line in your stead."

Daisy looked toward Darla, commenting, "Oh. Okay. Thanks Darla."

Strain went on, "I have assigned her to help you. I want you and Ms. Firkens to see this project through to completion. She has briefed me on her ideas for the story's premise and feels the deadline is still attainable. Do you have any questions or objections with my decision Ms. Zookes?"

"No, none that I can think of at the moment. Mr. Strain, I understand your decisions and I look forward to working with Darla. I do feel up to the task and want to see this project through."

"Good. Then I will leave you two alone to catch up and proceed with the project." Strain felt confident in his choice of asking Darla to assist Daisy. He knew the two women were friends and believed they would work well together. With his part of the business discussion finished, he said goodbye and wished Daisy a speedy recovery.

After he left Daisy said, "Well I guess it's business as usual," and the two started to laugh.

Glad to see Daisy looking and acting as her old self again, Darla shared some of her ideas.

She asked, "How about doing the adventure story with an endangered wild cat's angle?" She displayed the cat magazine from Daisy's apartment and some other research material she had collected. She continued, "I have been doing research about endangered cats. Do you know how many wild cats are in danger of becoming extinct?"

Baffled with this turn of events, Daisy thought it had to be a coincidence, because she hadn't mentioned a word about the province of Niv, Spotty, or anything about endangered species. Now, she wished more than ever for the pink notebook full of endangered species information. Her notes from the adventure into Niv would come in handy as they worked on the story together.

Daisy answered, "Tell me Darla, how did you get interested in this topic?"

Darla proceeded to share with Daisy the cat magazine article and how it sparked her interest. She said, "Since you have a genuine love for Aloewishish, I figured we could put something together in a short period of time. I didn't plan on becoming consumed with the plight of animals, it just happened. This study and research I have been doing has gotten under my skin. Do you have any knowledge about the predicament of the wild cats habitat?"

Daisy responded, "Why don't you fill me about the cats' predicament? I'm interested." The two spoke for hours and added to Darla's notes and rough outline for the story.

By the end of the week, Daisy's parents planned to return to Pennsylvania. Tulip would stay on a few more days to help Daisy resettle back into her apartment. Martha and Jonathan could see their daughter's strength returning, It became apparent, they were becoming more of a crowd than a need, as Paul assumed command of Daisy's well being. This pleased them. They were glad to have their daughter back alive and well. The time had come for them to return to Pennsylvania, their grandchildren, and the T & D Nursery.

With each passing day, Daisy's health improved. Later in the week, she wanted to wear something other than a boring hospital gown. She asked Paul to bring some clothes from her apartment. Daisy provided him with a list.

Paul surprised her when he returned with the listed items including an extra bag. Opening the extra bag, Daisy found Paul had packed the exact same outfit she had worn in Niv. The white shirt and khaki pants were neatly folded. They sat on top of the penny loafers and the delicate gold chain necklace. The pink notebook lay at the bottom of the bag.

" Paul, where did you find these items?"

"They were lying in a neat pile on your bed. You must

have placed them there before your accident. I thought you might want an extra outfit, so I brought them along too."

Daisy's hands shook as she opened the pink notebook. Inside on the front cover, Spotty had penned her a note with the yellow number-two pencil.

Dear Ms. Daisy,

You left in such a hurry, that you forgot your notebook. Sorry about the scratches I made with my talons on the front of the notebook, but you know how it is for me to carry things. I got permission from the King to bring back your things. I do hope these items find you well, happy, and rested. It had been a joy and pleasure to escort you around our beautiful province. Best to you on the adventure story.

Your friend from Begin Again Thoroughfare,

Spotty

Daisy couldn't believe it. Speechless, she looked up at Paul who had been watching her. Shaking her head in disbelief, she began to cradle the pink notebook. For a moment, she wondered about the yellow number-two pencil, but then dismissed it at her joy of having retrieved all of her notes from her unforgettable journey in a place called Niv.

Paul watched as Daisy looked over these items again and again. He wondered what had caused such a reaction. He could tell by her facial expression this notebook held a special meaning to her. He leaned forward and glanced someone's signature on the note.

He asked, "Is this note from a competitor of mine?"

She smiled reassuring Paul and said, "No need to worry Paul. This is from my friend Spotty." Rubbing her hands over the cover of the notebook where his talons had torn through and made grooves she said, "Honest Paul, Spotty isn't my type. You don't need to worry about him being a dating competitor." And then she laughed.

Paul didn't know what she laughed about, but he felt confidant Daisy had told him the truth. He excused himself and left to go to the cafeteria for a cup of coffee.

Daisy sat on her bed leafing through the notebook. She picked up the shoes and turned one of them over. When she did, out poured a small pile of sand. This brought a lump to Daisy's throat and she let out a sound of wonderment. It frightened her some to know where the sand came from, and it verified she had traveled to and had been on the distant Shores of Promise.

Chapter Twenty Six:

THE PLANS

Tulip returned home, leaving Daisy in the care of Darla and Paul. The two sisters said goodbye, cherishing their sisterhood and friendship even more since this traumatic event. Paul returned to work and continued to spend a lot of time with Daisy in the evening. In so doing he often saw Darla too.

For the next five weeks during her recuperation period, Daisy was permitted to work part-time at the Benson Building.

Wholeheartedly, Darla committed one hundred percent of her time to the researching and writing of this adventure story with Daisy. Darla became more passionate about the work each day as they dove deeper into the world of endangered and extinct species worldwide. She and Daisy worked on the story with fervor. They bonded over this new life's passion they were embarking upon.

As the weeks passed, the two wrote, researched, and redrafted the manuscript about an endangered wildcat. From time to time, Strain would check in on them, expecting an update for his contact Gloria Davenport of the Adolescents

Do Read Publications.

Daisy jumped on board with Darla's idea about creating the story about an endangered species wildcat getting lost in the jungle of buildings in New York City. The premise consisted of an adventure about a young boy befriending the cat and leading him to safety. Darla suggested, "Let's add an extra twist and weave endangered animal facts throughout the story line." Daisy agreed and utilized the pink notebook.

"I notice you often use notes when putting together your articles and stories," said Darla. Pointing to the pink notebook she asked, "So how did you accumulate this data?"

"Oh, I, uh, got some information for us to use from, uh, here and there. You know, just around." Her precious journey into Niv remained personal and private. Feeling vulnerable, she desired not to divulge this experience for fear of being scrutinized.

As the weeks passed, Darla became reacquainted with Paul's friend Zachary. The foursome would go out on dinner dates and take in a movie or two.

With the deadline fast approaching, Strain would meet with the two occupied writers for an ongoing update. What he read pleased him. As long as they kept him in the loop, he felt in control of the making of the story. He believed these two women would not fail to finish the project on time.

After Darla and Daisy submitted the completed adventure story, Gloria Davenport invited them to a luncheon. During the lunch date, she commended them on the remarkable job and asked, "Do you have any future plans to proceed with this subject matter?"

They shared their newfound passion for the wildlife survival and its worldwide loss of habitat.

Davenport said, "I have an inside lead with a reputable magazine firm specializing in endangered species. Would either of you be interested?"

Both spoke in unison expressing an affirmative response.

Davenport interjected, "I feel it would be a waste of time and talent if you two didn't follow your hearts' passion."

A few days later, the two submitted their resumes, along with a portfolio to the Danger n' X-Tinct publications manager. Mike J. Rhwalton, the executive manager, interviewed Daisy and Darla and hired them on the spot. Even though it would mean a cut in pay, both believed they had been destined for this new job. Their hearts had taken a turn with concern for the future of the animal kingdom. They didn't have to relocate, but the new job required travel time due to its mobile assignments.

Sorry to see the two women resign but understanding their success, Ted Strain had his secretary arrange a small reception on their last day of work at the Hannah and Rhutkers JC Publishing Company. Strain knew they would be missed within their department. The small going away bash took place in the eleventh-story break room. Strain's secretary arranged for complimentary cake, punch, and coffee to be served.

Strain had invited Tom Nimbleton to the break room gathering. This had been one of those special times Tom's son, along with his wife and Sissy, visited him at the office. Tom took his son with him to the break room for a piece of cake. When Tom and his son entered the break room, Daisy bumped into the little boy and knocked a picture book he carried under his arm. She stooped to pick it up and gave a startled cry when she saw a picture of a Northern Spotted Owl on the cover of the child's book. Tom apologized for his son's mishap and introduced himself and his son Braden to Daisy.

Daisy had difficulty focusing on what Tom was saying as somehow she felt connected to the little boy. The little boy smiled and thanked her for picking up his treasured book.

Tom spoke to Daisy and wished her well. Ted came over and broke the spell of the moment, stating that it had been Tom who had found her lying unconscious in the stairwell on that fateful day. She thanked Tom for his kindness and remained dumbstruck as she watched Tom and his son exit the break room She noticed that the little boy held tight to the picture book of the owl. For some reason, Daisy knew she had met him before, but failed to remember where.

Six months after Daisy's accident, Paul and his friend, Zachary invited the two women on a mission trip. They were going to hike the tallest free-standing mountain in the world, Mount Kilmanjaro, located in east Africa. The two women jumped at this opportunity to explore and take great photos for future articles.

At her last health checkup, Dr. Kabintzol gave Daisy a clean bill of health. He saw no reason she couldn't hike up the mountain. She and Darla packed for the big outing and joined the group of mission-minded enthusiasts on a journey to east Africa and Mount Kilmanjaro. The journey to Africa took two days due to delays. Each person had been permitted only a limited amount of gear.

Their mission group consisted of sixteen men, women, and teenagers. Each journeyed up to the gorgeous summit of this long trek with a personal goal in mind. The bulk of them were raising funds in support of a world's mission outreach to help the less fortunate. Every evening, Daisy and Darla sat around the campfire listening to the group share a belief and faith in their King. When the two would retreat to sleep in their tent, they would decipher and assimilate what they heard from the campfire discussions.

Before the trek up the mountain began, Daisy had confided to Paul some of the things she experienced in the province of Niv during her comatose state. Now in her tent, she began to share a few of these adventurous moments with Darla. On the fourth morning at breakfast, Darla and Daisy were convinced they wanted to render their lives in service of the King the group spoke about. They asked to meet with the spiritual leader of the group. In their thirst for what they were learning from the others and the new life they were leading, the two girls asked, "How can we walk in faith like Paul, Zachary, and the others?"

Seeing that they were earnest, the leader explained how they could know the King and become one of his followers. For Daisy and Darla it became a mountaintop experience before they even reached the summit.

That day on their Mount Kilmanjaro climb, they accepted the plan laid out for spiritual freedom and surrendered their hearts to the King of Kings. The group celebrated with a breakfast of hotcakes and coffee with their newfound friends and believers-Darla and Daisy. Paul and Zachary's hearts swelled with pride, as they knew this had been a big step for Daisy and Darla. These two tenderhearted women were aspiring writers who wanted to make a difference in the world.

The morning's reading around the campfire had been Jeremiah 29:11: "For I know the plans I have for you," declares the Lord, "plans to prosper you and not to harm you, plans to give you hope and a future." It fit the moment well.

Paul, Daisy, Zachary and Darla cemented their relationships together on the Mountain of Kilmanjaro. Throughout their entire lives, the two couples would remain friends, bound by this sacred experience. Daisy and Darla continued their passionate work for endangered species throughout the world. By shedding the King's light within each article they wrote, they wove a message of hope. Above all, Daisy never forgot the awesome journey into the province of Niv. This is where her fairytale life ended and her life into reality began.

At the Benson Building on 10 Peridion Street, the night janitor Ian Markus of the Hannah and Rhutkers JC Publishing Company cleaned the east stairwell. Working on the ninth floor landing, he found a yellow number-two pencil wedged in the corner. He picked up the pencil. It looked like a good pencil, perfect for him to use to fill out his evening paperwork at the end of his shift. He placed the yellow number-two pencil into his top blue-green shirt pocket and finished his duties. Where this pencil travels on from here is another story for another time.

REFERENCES:

AURORA (ASTRONOMY)

From Wikipedia, The Free Encyclopedia
http://en.wikipedia.org/wiki/Aurora_(astronomy)

BETA BLOCKERS

MedicineNet.com 'We bring doctors knowledge to you.'
http://www.medicinenet.com/beta_blockers/article.htm

CARDIOPULMONARY RESUSCITATION (CPR)

http://en.wikipedia.org/wiki/Cardiopulmonary_resuscitation

CULTURES AND HISTORY NOTES FROM THE PAST;

Onieda Indians
http://oneida-nation.net/notes.html

DEBORAH THE PROPHETESS AND JUDGE

ESSORTMENT - Information and advice you want to know
http://www.essortment.com/deborahjudge_rsui.htm
http://www.ldolphin.org/Deborah.html

ENDANGERED SPECIES

http://www.enchantedlearning.com/subjects/

Oregon Silverspot Butterfly, Northern Spotted Owl, Hawaiian Goose, African Elephant, Oryx, Gazelle, Gorilla, Jackass Penquin, Okapi, Orangutan, Aye-aye

http://www.birds.cornell.edu/AllAboutBirds/BirdGuide/Song_Sparrow.html#sound
Song Sparrow

http://money.cnn.com/2008/02/17/news/companies/bees_ice-cream/index.htm?postversion=2008021712
Honey Bee

Articlehttp://www.panda.org/about_wwf/what_we_do/species/our_solutions/endangered_species/index.cfm
Marine Turtle

www.nrcan-rncan.gc.ca, Last Modified: 2007-03-06 08:52:40
News related articles from the Atlantic Forestry Centre.
The Butternut

EVALUATING THE COMATOSE PATIENT

http://www.postgradmed.com/issues/2002/02_02/malik.htm

HOUSE PAGE PROGRAM

http://www.house.gov/platts/pdfs/page-program-about.pdf

JOKES

Jokelopedia, compiled by Ilana Weitzman, Eva Blank, Alison Benjamin and Rosanne Green, Illustrated by Mike Wright, Copyright @2000 by Sommersvile House.

MOUNT KILIMANJARO

http://www.tanzaniaparks.com/kili.htm

SCRIPTURE REFERENCES

Jeremiah 29:11 (New International Version) "For I know the plans I have for you," declares the Lord, "plans to prosper you and not to harm you, plans to give you hope and a future."

Philippians 4:8 (Contemporary English Version)
"My friends, keep your minds on whatever is true, pure, right, holy, friendly, and proper. Don't ever stop thinking on what is truly worthwhile and worthy of praise."

REVELATION 21:15 – 21 (NEW INTERNATIONAL VERSION)

15The angel who talked with me had a measuring rod of gold to measure the city, its gates and its walls. 16The city was laid out like a square, as long as it was wide. He measured the city with the rod and found it to be 12,000 stadia[a]in length, and as wide and high as it is long. 17He measured its wall and it was 144 cubits[b] thick,[c] by man's measurement, which the angel was using. 18The wall was made of jasper, and the city of pure gold, as pure as glass. 19The foundations of the city walls were decorated with every kind of precious stone. The first foundation was jasper, the second sapphire, the third chalcedony, the fourth emerald, 20the fifth sardonyx, the sixth carnelian, the seventh chrysolite, the eighth beryl, the ninth topaz, the tenth chrysoprase, the eleventh jacinth, and the twelfth amethyst.[d] 21The twelve gates were twelve pearls, each gate made of a single pearl. The great street of the city was of pure gold, like transparent glass.

2 CHRONICLES 1:15 (NEW INTERNATIONAL VERSION)

15 The king made silver and gold as common in Jerusalem as stones, and cedar as plentiful as sycamore-fig trees in the foothills.

GENESIS 1:14-18 (NEW INTERNATIONAL VERSION)

14 And God said, "Let there be lights in the expanse of the sky to separate the day from the night, and let them serve as signs to mark seasons and days and years, 15 and let them be lights in the expanse of the sky to give light on the earth." And it was so. 16 God made two great lights—the greater light to govern the day and the lesser light to govern the night. He also made the stars. 17 God set them in the expanse of the sky to give light on the earth, 18 to govern the day and the night, and to separate light from darkness. And God saw that it was good. 19 And there was evening, and there was morning—the fourth day.

PSALM 19: 1-3
(NEW INTERNATIONAL VERSION)

For the director of music. A psalm of David. 1 The heavens declare the glory of God; the skies proclaim the work of his hands. 2 Day after day they pour forth speech; night after night they display knowledge. 3 There is no speech or language where their voice is not heard.

SPANISH CONQUISTADORS

http://www.elizabethan-era.org.uk/spanish-conquistadors.htm

SURRENDER ALL

Words: Judson W. Van DeVenter, 1896:
http://www.cyberhymnal.org/htm/i/s/isurrend.htm
We Surrender All
We Surrender All
All to thee our Precious King
We Surrender All

SYCAMORE FIG

http://baheyeldin.com/places/egypt/sycamore-fig-an-egyptian-tree-and-fruit-mulberry-fig-egyptian-sycamore-cumbez.html
Old Testament and the New Testament (Amos 7:14, Jeremiah 24:2, Luke 19:4).

WARRIOR NAMES

http://www.lowchensaustralia.com/names/warriornames.htm
http://www.babynamesworld.com/search.php?p=category&e=cat&i_category=asian&s_gender5=3&page=4#continue
1 Chronicles 11:20-21 New International Version

Wise Geek - WHAT IS A DEFIBRILLATOR

http://www.wisegeek.com/what-is-a-defibrillator.htm
PostGraduate Medicine Online Symposium

YORUBA LANGUAGE

http://en.wikipedia.org/wiki/Yoruba_language

ABOUT THE AUTHOR

JANICE BLAIR resides in Northwestern Pennsylvania near her large extended family. However, she and her husband travel often to Pittsburgh visiting their two married daughters and their husbands. Also, she has traveled extensively, with her most memorable trip being a 10-day excursion throughout Israel.

Janice is an Air Force Veteran and she is professionally educated as an administrative assistant. She gave her heart to The Lord in 1980, and remains faithful to bible study and fellowship with other believers.

Not waiting for others or the government, she believes reform starts with her. Her goal in life is to encourage others. She does this by providing positive messages to help people overcome challenges within their daily lives. She is a firm believer that 'What you feed grows and what you starve dies.'

FEEDING ENCOURAGING WORDS

TO MOST EVERYONE WE MEET CAN HELP

RID THE WORLD OF RESENTMENT,

HATE, ANGER, AND DISAPPOINTMENT,

WHICH CAN BE FOUND IN ANY TOWN

IN THE WORLD. ENJOY THE BOOK. I DID.

JANICE BLAIR

WA